Stories from Down Under

*Nine short stories from Australia
and New Zealand*

edited and annotated
by
Karin Ikas & David Carter

Langenscheidt

Berlin · München · Wien · Zürich · New York

Viewfinder

Literature

Unterrichtsmaterial für die Sekundarstufe II

Stories from Down Under

Herausgeber:
Prof. Dr. Dr. h.c. Peter Freese

Bearbeitung:
Dr. Karin Ikas, M.A.
Prof. David Carter

Umwelthinweis: Gedruckt auf chlorfrei gebleichtem Papier

1. Auflage 2004

© 2004 Langenscheidt ELT GmbH, München

Printed in Germany

ISBN 3-526-50798-8

Contents

Introduction

This Viewfinder Literature volume presents several important and influential short stories of leading Indigenous and non-Indigenous writers[1] from Australia and New Zealand together with concise background information to introduce the reader to the diversity and richness of two of the most exciting and rapidly expanding Commonwealth Literatures.

The literatures of Australia and New Zealand can also be thought of as "new" literatures.[2] Settlement by Europeans and other non-Indigenous immigrants is a relatively recent phenomenon and in each country writers have had to think about their relationship to English or European cultures and to the creation of a new culture in their new land. In this process the relationship between Indigenous and non-Indigenous peoples becomes a major theme. Even in an age of global communication, much about Australia and New Zealand remains unfamiliar to the rest of the world. Fiction provides a unique opportunity for readers to "listen in" to the stories Australians and New Zealanders have told themselves and others about their land, their society and their history.

Australia and New Zealand share many features. Both are lands occupied by Indigenous peoples – the Aborigines and Torres Strait Islanders in Australia, the Maori in New Zealand. These lands were settled by the British in the late 18th and early 19[th]c. In both places settlement involved the often violent dispossession of the Indigenous peoples from their lands. Race relations and land claims remain important factors in both societies. Both countries were colonies of Britain and both retain a formal link to the monarchy although this has little significance in the day to day running of their political systems or diplomatic relations. For the new settlers in both countries, living far distant from homelands in Britain, Ireland or Europe, the coming to terms with a new land, a new society and a new identity provided major themes in literature and other forms of cultural expression.

---

1 It is common practice in Australia and New Zealand now to give a capital letter for Indigenous and also to replace the often-used term "white" (to denote the opposite) by other expressions such as "non-Indigenous," Anglophone and Asian, Australians of European and Asian ethnicity, etc.).

2 To learn more about different New Literatures in English see Christa Jansohn, ed., *Companion to the New Literatures in English* (Berlin: Erich Schmidt Verlag, 2002). Consult this collection also for an annotated bibliography of different reference books (including Australian and New Zealand Literatures). For more information on the respective critical approaches to these literatures in the array of Colonial, Postcolonial and Cultural Studies check in particular Elleke Boemer, *Colonial & Postcolonial Literature* (Oxford and New York: Opus, 1995). Also Bill Ashcroft, Gareth Griffiths and Helen Tiffin, *The Empire Writes Back: Theory and Practice in Post-Colonial Literatures* (London and New York: Routledge, 1989) and Michael Mitchell, ed., *The Postcolonial Experience: Decolonizing the Mind* (München: Langenscheidt-Longman, 1995).

As ties to Britain have greatly diminished since the 1960s, Australia and New Zealand have undergone major economic and cultural change. They have redefined themselves in terms of their geographic location, as Asian-Pacific nations, and as multicultural or multiracial societies.

There are nonetheless important differences between the two countries: Aborigines in Australia, for example, comprise between 2-3% of the population; the Maori population in New Zealand make up almost 15%. Immigration has been a much greater influence on the Australian population. Together these factors have led some commentators to talk of *multi*-culturalism in Australia and *bi*-culturalism in New Zealand. The first British settlement of the Australian continent was to establish a convict colony, but this was never part of New Zealand's history. Australia has a very large land mass and a very distinctive natural environment, most of which is dry and presents a serious challenge both to agriculture and human habitation. It is therefore a highly urbanised nation. New Zealand's climate and landscape, by contrast, in many respects resembles a European environment. Australia's larger population has also enabled it to play an important role as a "middle power" in international affairs, especially since World War II.[3]

These points of similarity and difference suggest some of the themes we can look for when reading short stories from the two countries: the relationships between different cultures, settlement in and immigration to new lands and new communities, attitudes to nature and the environment, and the search for identity on the local, national and international levels.

Australian literature, like Australian cinema, might now be called truly international. Certain Australian writers are now widely known, at least in the English-speaking world. Novelist Patrick White was awarded the Nobel Prize for literature in 1973. Peter Carey has twice won the Booker Prize, the most prestigious international award for a novel (in 1988 for *Oscar and Lucinda*, also made into a feature film; in 2001, for *The True History of the Kelly Gang*). Thomas Keneally won the Booker Prize in 1982 for *Schindler's Ark*, later made into the film *Schindler's List*. David Malouf, novelist, short story writer and poet, was awarded the first International IMPAC Dublin Prize (1996) and the French Prix Baudelaire, for *Remembering Babylon*, plus the 2000 Neustadt International Prize. Poet

---

3   The former Australian Foreign Minister, Gareth Evans, described Australia as a "middle power nation" in a speech in Tokyo in November 1993. The characteristic feature of the diplomacy of middle power nations (i.e. medium-sized countries in terms of their economic or military influence) is that they form alliances with other like-minded nations. They can potentially influence international events without involving the superpowers.

Les Murray won the T. S. Eliot Prize in 1997. New Zealand novelist Keri Hulme was awarded the Booker Prize for her novel *The Bone People* in 1985.

In the colonial period in both countries, short fiction developed as an important literary form. With a population too small to support a regular book publishing industry, fiction writers depended upon newspapers and magazines for publication. This also meant that they wrote mostly for a local audience and so local themes and settings became popular, although of course many writers stayed with themes and styles already familiar from English books and magazines which their audience also knew.

With the influence of realism in literature in the late nineteenth century, the short story became an ideal form for stories seeking to capture local realities, e.g. life in the bush in Australia or agricultural communities in New Zealand. This was also a period when nationalism became an important influence. Henry Lawson and Price Warung belong to this era. Writers sought to show what was *distinctive* about their land or society, what made it unique.

These influences remained strong in both countries from the 1880s through to the 1960s (see for example John Morrison's story in this volume), although from the 1930s on modernist influences were also important. This was a significant period in Australia for women writers, including Eleanor Dark, Christina Stead, Katharine Susannah Prichard, and Marjorie Barnard. New Zealand's Katherine Mansfield established an international reputation as a modern writer, living in England and Europe.

Stories from this period were mainly concerned with defining the nature of "white" identity in Australia and New Zealand, although Roderick Finlayson's story from 1930s New Zealand suggests the role that race relations would come to play in both countries. By the 1970s the relations between the settler populations and the Indigenous populations had become a major political issue. Aboriginal and Maori writers in English were making their presence felt (including Witi Ihamaera in NZ), and non-Indigenous writers began to see race relations as crucial to a true understanding of the nation's history and the moral basis of its social relations. Thea Astley, David Malouf and Gerald Murnane all reflect on this unavoidable issue.

The range of voices in the two literatures has become very diverse in the last twenty years, reflecting the influences of immigration, on the one hand, and of internationalisation or globalisation, on the other. Lily Brett writes from the experience of one group of migrants to Australia, European Jews. Italian, Greek, Chinese, Vietnamese and writers from many other ethnic groups have also contributed to contemporary Australian literature. Both countries have witnessed strong periods of cultural growth and confidence since the 1970s.

Australian and New Zealand literatures have certain aspects in common with those of other white settler/immigrant societies such as Canada and even the USA. An Australian critic recently wrote that "the great Australian [and we can add NZ] themes – dispossession and alienation, racist violence and belligerent nationalism, colonisation and post-colonialism, war and migration, industrialisation and urbanisation, the redefinition of gender roles and expectations – are also the major themes of international modern history."[4]

But their relatively recent histories, their colonial and "post-colonial" status, their geographical location, and their unique cultural and ethnic compositions, mean that the literatures of the two countries have distinctive stories to tell. They provide a rich and contrasting experience which this book invites you to enjoy.

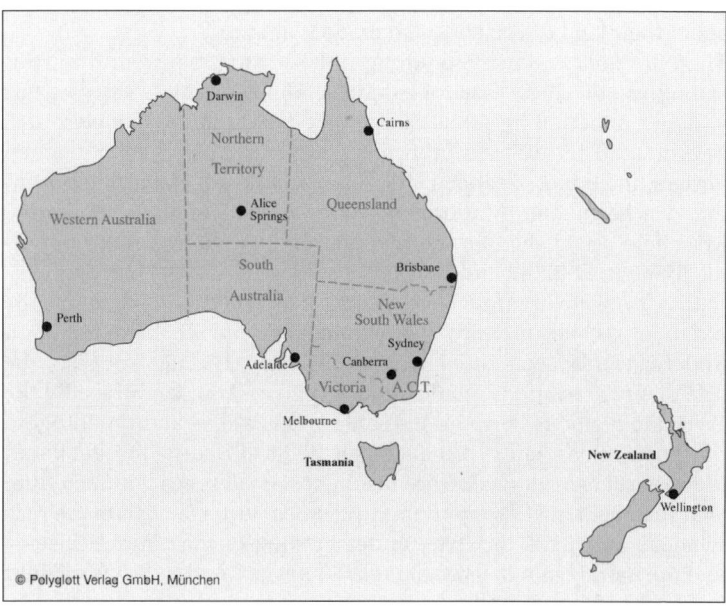

© Polyglott Verlag GmbH, München

4   Robin Gerster, "Cobbers and Cobblers. Review of Richard Nile, ed., *The Australian Legend and its Discontents* (University of Queensland Press, 2000)," in: *Australian Book Review* 222 (August 2000): 14-16, 14.

1 | Price Warung

Price Warung was born William Astley in Liverpool, England, in 1855. He was brought to Melbourne by his family in 1859, and worked as a freelance journalist in NSW, Victoria and Tasmania in the years 1875-1890 before settling in Sydney. He adopted the name "Price Warung" as his pen-name. Warung became famous as a writer through his stories of Australia's convict days which were published in the Sydney *Bulletin* magazine in the early 1890s. This was Australia's most influential magazine. It published most of the major writers of this period including Henry Lawson (see the next story) and A. B. Paterson (who wrote the words to Australia's best-known song, "Waltzing Matilda").

Price Warung did not himself experience the period of the convict colony in Australia. The transportation of convicts to NSW ceased in 1840 and to all the eastern states of Australia by 1852. However, there would still have been survivors of the convict system alive at the time he began writing his stories. While still young, he developed a strong interest in Australia's past and he claimed to have spent twenty years researching the background for his stories of early Australian life.

It is important when reading "How Muster-Master Stoneman Earned his Breakfast" to remember that Warung is describing a period long before the time he was writing ("55 years ago" the story says). The story recreates the past convict system for contemporary readers in the 1890s. In doing so, although it provides very realistic detail, it does not just present a neutral description but uses literary techniques to create a vivid, dramatic picture of the cruelty and inhumanity of the system.

The "muster station" is an area where convicts were gathered together to be given their work duties or punishment. Stoneman is the officer in charge, the "Muster-*Master.*" The story is set in Tasmania (then Van Diemen's Land) where the conditions for convicts were often extremely harsh. Historical accounts suggest that for most convicts life was not as harsh as shown in this story, but Warung wants to emphasize one interpretation of the convict system as strongly as possible.

The most important literary technique Warung uses in the story is irony. Even the title is ironic: Stoneman feels that he has "earned his breakfast" but our reaction is likely to be one of shock and outrage, for his morning's work has been to order the convict flogged almost to death before being hanged. Reading carefully we can note the use of irony throughout the story: for example, he uses terms such as "the mild discipline" of the "genial and loving motherland" to describe the cruelties of the system of imprisonment and punishment established by England, which condemns people like Convict Glancy rather than "loving" them.

Although Convict Glancy is shown to be violent (he kills the Overseer and then the prison warder), the focus of the story is on the violence and cruelty of the system. This cruelty is not just a matter of physical punishment but also the pettiness and absurdity of the bureaucracy, the rules and regulations of the system which give power to the officials and trap the convicts. Here the flogging and rubbing salt into Glancy's back are meaningless because he is to be executed straight after, but it satisfies the Muster-Master's sense of power and authority. Throughout the story Warung also exaggerates the pompous language of the system. Despite Glancy's crimes we can see him as a human being with feelings, but for the system he is just a number.

For much of the nineteenth century Australians were ashamed of the founding of their colony as a convict settlement. By the 1890s, however, attitudes had begun to change. Warung's stories express these new attitudes by suggesting that the convicts were mostly innocent victims of a cruel system, a system which reflected Britain's oppressive colonial rule. Perhaps this wasn't strictly accurate, but it was an attractive story for Australians to believe. Note that Glancy was originally jailed and sent to Australia merely for stealing a silk handkerchief from a rich man, a "swell." It is the system which has turned him into a cruel murderer.

HOW MUSTER-MASTER STONEMAN EARNED HIS BREAKFAST

An unpretentious building of rough-hewn stone standing in the middle of a small, stockaded enclosure. A doorway in the wall of the building facing the entrance-gate to the yard. To the left of the doorway, a glazed window of the ordinary size. To its right a paneless aperture, so low and narrow that were the four upright and two transverse bars which grate it doubled in thickness no interstice would be left for the admission of light or air to the interior. Behind the bars – a face.

Sixteen hours hence that face will look its last upon the world which has stricken it countless cruel blows. In a corner of the enclosure the executioner's hand is even now busy stitching into a shapeless cap, a square of grey serge. Tomorrow the same hand will use the cap to hood the face, as one of the few simple preliminaries to swinging the carcase to which the face is attached from the rude platform now in course of erection against the stockade fence and barely 20 yards in front of the stone building.

The building is the gaol – locally known as the "cage" – of Oatlands, a small township in the midlands of Van Diemen's Land, which has gradually grown up round a convict "muster-station", established by Governor Davey. The time is five o'clock on a September evening, 55 years ago. At nine o'clock on the following morning, Convict Glancy, No. 17,927, transportee ex ship Pestonjee Bomanjee (second trip), originally under sentence for seven years for the theft of a silk handkerchief from a London "swell", will suffer the extreme penalty of the law for having, in an intemperate moment, objected to the mild discipline with which a genial and loving motherland had sought to correct his criminal tendencies. In other words, Convict Glancy, metaphorically goaded by the wordy insults and literally by the bayonet-tip of one of his motherland's reformatory agents – to wit, Road-gang Overseer James Jones – had scattered JJ's brains over a good six square yards of metalled roadway. The deed has been rapturously applauded by Glancy's fellow-gangers, all of whom had the inclination, but lacked the courage, to wield the crowbar that has been the means of erasing this particular tyrant's name from the pay-sheets of His Britannic Majesty's Colonial Penal Establishment. Nevertheless and notwithstanding such tribute of appreciation, H.B.M.'s colonial representatives, police, judicial and gubernatorial, have thought it rather one to be censured and have, accordingly, left Convict Glancy for execution.

40　　This decision of the duly-constituted authorities Convict Glancy has somewhere irrelevantly (as it will seem to us at this enlightened day) acknowledged by a fervent "Thank God!" – an ejaculation rendered the more remarkable by the fact that never before in his convict history had he linked the name of the Deity with any expression
45　of gratitude for the many blessings enjoyed by him in that state of penal servitude to which it had pleased the same Deity to call him. On the contrary, he had constantly indulged in maledictions on his fate and on his Maker. He had resolutely cursed the benignant forces with which the System and the King's Regulations had sur-
50　rounded him, and he had failed to reverence as he ought the triangles, the gang-chains, the hominy, the prodding bayonet, and the other things which would have conduced to his reformation had he but manifested a more humble and obedient spirit. No wonder, therefore, as Chaplain Ford said, that it has come about that he has
55　qualified for the capital doom.

　　Upon this doom, in so far as it could be represented by the gallows, Convict Glancy was now gazing with an unflinching eye. On this September evening he stands at his cell-window looking on half-a-dozen brown-clothed figures handling saw, and square, and
60　hammer, as they fix in the earth two sturdy uprights, and to those a projecting cross-beam; as they bind the two with a solid tie-piece of knotless hardwood; as they build a narrow platform of planks around the gallows-tree; as they fasten a rope to the notched end of the cross-beam; and as they slope to the edge of the planks, ten feet
65　from the ground, a rude ladder. All the drowsy afternoon he had watched the working party, though Chaplain Ford had stood by his side droning of the grace which had been withheld from him in life, but might still be his in death. He had felt interested, had Convict Glancy, in these preparations for the event in which he was to act
70　such a prominent part on the morrow. He had even laughed at the grim humour of one of the brown-garbed workers who, when the warder's eye was off him, had gone through the pantomime of noosing the rope-end round his own neck – a little joke which contributed much to the (necessarily noiseless) delight of the rest of the
75　gang.

　　Altogether, Convict Glancy reflected as dusk fell, and the working party gathered up their tools, and the setting sun tipped the bayonets of the guard with a diamond iridescence, that he had spent many a duller afternoon. If the Chaplain had only held his tongue,
80　the time would have passed with real pleasantness. He said as much to the good man as the latter remarked to the warder on duty in the cell that he would look in again after supper.

"You may save yourself the trouble, sir," quoth, respectfully enough, Convict Glancy. "You have spoilt my last afternoon. Don't spoil my last night!"

Chaplain Ford winced at the words. He was still comparatively new to the work of spiritually superintending a hundred or so monsters who looked upon the orthodox hell as a place where residence would be pleasantly recreative after Port Arthur Settlement and Norfolk Island; and the time lay still in the future when, being completely embruted, he would come to regard it as a very curious circumstance indeed that Christ had omitted eulogistic reference to the System from the Sermon on the Mount. Consequently he winced and sighed, not so much – to do him justice – at the utter depravity of Convict Glancy as at his own inability to reach the reprobate's heart. But he took the hint; he mournfully said he would not return that evening, but would be with the prisoner by half-past 5 o'clock in the morning.

II

When Chaplain Ford entered the enclosure immediately before the hour he had named, he at once understood, from the excitement manifested by a group assembled in front of the "cage", that something was amiss. Voices were uttering fearful words, impetuously, almost shriekingly, and hands swung lanterns – the grey dawn had not yet driven the darkness from the stockade – and brandished muskets furiously. A very brief space of time served to inform the reverend functionary what had gone wrong.

Convict Glancy had made his escape, having previously murdered, with the victim's own bayonet, the warder who had been told-off to watch him during the night. This latter circumstance was, of course, unfortunate, but alone it would not have created the excitement, for the murder of prison-officials was a common enough occurrence. It was the other thing that galled the gesticulating and blaspheming group. That a prisoner, fettered with ten-pound irons, should have broken out of gaol on the very eve of his execution – why, it was calculated to shake the confidence of the Comptroller-General himself in the infallibility and perfect righteousness of the System. And, popular and authoritative belief in the System once shattered, where would they be?

The murdered man had gone on duty at 10 o'clock, and very shortly afterwards he must have met with his fate. How Glancy had obtained possession of the bayonet could only be conjectured. As was the custom during the day or two preceding a convict's execution, he had been left unmanacled, and ironed with double leg-chains only. Thus his hands were free to perpetrate the deed once he grasped the weapon. Glancy, on his escape, had taken the instrument with him, but there was no doubt that he had inflicted death with it, the wound in the dead man's breast being obviously caused by the regulation bayonet. Possibly the sentinel had nodded, and then a violent wrench of the prisoner's wrist and a sudden stab had extended his momentary slumber into an eternal sleep. The bayonet had been used by Glancy to prise up a flooring-flag, and to scoop out an aperture under the wall, the base-stones of which, following the slipshod architecture of the time, rested on the surface and were not sunk into the ground.

The work of excavation must have taken the convict several hours, and must have been conducted as noiselessly as the manner of committing the crime itself. A solitary warder occupied the outer guardroom, but he asserted that he had heard no sound except the exchange of whistle-signals between the dormitory guard at the convict-barracks (a quarter-of-mile away at the rear of the gaol-stockade) and the military patrol. The night routine of the "cage" did not insist upon the whistle-signal between the men on duty, but they passed a simple "All's well" every hour. And this the guard-room-warder maintained he had done with the officer inside the condemned cell, the response being given in a low tone, from consideration, so the former thought, for the sleeping convict so soon to die. Of course, if this man was to be believed, Glancy must have uttered the words. It was not the first time the signal which should have been given by a prison officer had been made by his convict murderer.

The murder was discovered on the arrival of the relief watch at five o'clock. The last "All's well" was exchanged at four. Consequently the escapee had less than an hour's start. The scaling of the stockade would not be difficult even for a man in irons, and one in the bush an experienced hand would soon find a method of fracturing the links.

It must be admitted that this contumacious proceeding of Convict Glancy was most vexatious. Under-Sheriff Ropewell, now soundly reposing at the township inn, would be forthcoming at 9 o'clock with his Excellency's warrant in his hand to demand from Muster-Master Stoneman the body of one James Glancy, and Muster-Master Stoneman would have to apologise for his inability to produce the said body. The difficulty was quite unprecedented, and Stoneman, as he stood in the midst of his minions, groaned audibly at the prospect of having to do the thing most abhorrent to the official mind – establish a precedent.

"Such a thing was never heard of!" he cried. "A man to bolt just when he was to be turned off? And the d–d hypocrite tried to make his Honor and all of us think that he was only too happy to be scragged. It's too d–d bad!"

It certainly did seem peculiar that Glancy, who had apparently much rejoiced at the contemplation of his early decease, should give leg-bail just when he was to realise his wishes. He had told the judges that "he was glad they were going to kill him right off instead of by inches", and yet he had voluntarily thrown off the noose when it was virtually round his neck. Was it the mere contrariness of the convict nature that prompted the escape? Or, was it the innate love of life that becomes stronger as the benefits of living become fewer and fewer? Had the craving for existence and for freedom surged over his despair and recklessness at the eleventh hour?

Such were the enquiries which Chaplain Ford put to himself as, horrified, he took in the particulars of No. 17,927's crowning enormities from the hubbub of the group.

"Damn it!" said the Muster-Master at last, "we are losing time. The devil can't have gone far with those ten-pounders on him. We'll have to put the regulars on the track as well as our own men. Warder Briggs, report to Captain White at the barracks, and –"

Muster-Master Stoneman stopped short. Through the foggy air there came the familiar sound as of a convict dragging his irons. What could it be? No prisoners had been as yet loosed from the dormitory. Whence could the noise proceed?

Clink – clank – s-sh – dr-g-g – clink – clank – dr-g-g. The sound drew nearer, and Convict Glancy turned in at the enclosure gateway – unescorted. He had severed the leg-chain at the link which connected with the basil of the left anklet, but had not taken the trouble to remove the other part of the chain. Thus, while he could take his natural pace with his left foot, he dragged the fetters behind his right leg.

A moment of hushed surprise, and then three or four men rushed towards him. The first who touched him he felled with a blow.

"Not yet," said he, grimly. "I give myself up, Mr Stoneman – you don't take me! I give myself up – you ain't going to get ten quid[1] for taking me." And then Convict Glancy laughed, and held out his hands for the handcuffs. He laughed more heartily as the subordinate hirelings of the System threw themselves upon him like hounds on their prey.

"No need to turn out the sodgers now, Muster-Master – not till nine o'clock." Once more his hideous laugh rang through the yards. "You had an easier job than you expected, hadn't you, Stoneman, old cove?"

Muster-Master Stoneman had been surprised into silence and into an unusual abstinence from blasphemy by the re-appearance – quite unprecedented under the circumstances! – of the doomed wretch. But the desperado's jeering tones whipped him into speech.

"Curse you!" he yelled. "I'll teach you to laugh on the other side of your mouth presently. You'd better have kept away." He literally foamed in his mad anger.

"Do you think I couldn't have stopped away if I'd wanted to, having got clear?" A lofty scorn rang out in the words. "But do you think I was going to run away when I was so near Freedom as that?" And the wretch jerked his manacled hands in the direction of the gallows. "You d–d fool!"

No one spoke for a full half-minute. Then: "Why did you break gaol then?" asked the Muster-Master.

"Because I wanted to spit on Jones' grave!" was the reply.

III

Muster-Master Stoneman was as good as his word. Death couldn't drive the smile from Glancy's face. That could only be done by one thing – the lash.

When next the Muster-Master spoke it was to order the prisoner a double ration of cocoa and bread. And, "Briggs," he continued, "while he is getting it, see that the triangles are rigged."

"The triangles, sir!" exclaimed Officer Briggs and Convict Glancy together.

"I said the triangles, and I mean the triangles. No. 17,927 has broken gaol, and as Muster-Master of this station, and governor of this gaol, and as a magistrate of the territory, I can give him 750 lashes for escaping. But as he has to go through another little ceremony this morning I'll let him off with a 'canary'" – (a hundred lashes.)[2]

"You surely cannot mean it, sir!" exclaimed Parson Ford.

"Mean it, sir! By G–, I'll show you I mean it," replied the M.M., whose blaspheming no presence restrained save that of his official superiors. "Give him the cocoa. Warder Tuff, give the doctor my compliments, and tell him his attendance is required here. Tell him he'd better bring his smelling-salts – they may be wanted," he sneered in conclusion.

"You devil!" cried Glancy. The reckless grin passed away, and his face faded to the pallor of the death he was so soon to die.

As Master-Muster Stoneman turned on his heel to prepare the warrant for the flogging, he looked at his watch. It was half-past six.

At seven o'clock the first lash from the cat-o'-nine-tails fell upon Convict Glancy's back.

At 7.30 his groaning and bleeding body, which had received the full hundred of flaying stripes, lay on the pallet of the cell where he had murdered the night-guard but a few hours before.

At eight o'clock Executioner Johnson entered the cell. "I've brought yer sumthink to 'arden yer, Glancy, ol' man. I'll rub it in, an' it'll help yer to keep up." So tender a sympathy inspired Mr Johnson's words that anyone not knowing him would have thought he was the bearer of some priceless balsam. But Convict Glancy knew him; and, maddened by pain though he was, had still sensibility enough left to make a shuddering resistance to the hangman as he proceeded to rub into the gashed flesh a handful of coarse salt. "By the Muster-Master's orders, sonny," soothingly remarked Johnson. "To 'arden yer."

At 8.45 Under-Sheriff Ropewell, who had been apprised while at breakfast of the murder and escape, appeared on the scene escorted by his javelin-men. This gentleman, too, had been greatly perplexed by Convict Glancy's proceedings. "Really it was most inconsiderate of the man," he said to the Muster-Master. "I do not know whether I ought to proceed to execution, pending his trial for this second murder."

"Oh," said the latter functionary – flicking with his handkerchief from his coat-sleeve as he spoke a drop of Convict Glancy's blood that had fallen there from a reflex swirl of the lash, "I think your duty is clear. You must hang him at nine o'clock, and try him afterwards for the last crime."

And as Convict Glancy, per Pestonjee Bomanjee (second), No. 17,927, was punctually hanged at 9.5, it is to be presumed that the Under-Sheriff had accepted this solution of the difficulty.

At 10.15 a mass of carrion having been huddled into a shell, and certain formalities, which in the estimation of the System served as efficiently as a coroner's inquest, having been duly attended to, Muster-Master Stoneman bethought himself that he had not breakfasted.

"I'll see you later, Mr Ropewell," he said, as the latter was endorsing the Governor's warrant with the sham verdict: "I'm going to breakfast. I think I've earned it this morning."

---

[1] "Ten quid" – The reward of ten pounds paid by Government on the re-capture of an escaped prisoner.

[2] Muster-Master Stoneman had doubtless in his mind's eye when he made this remark the decision of a Sydney Court which had legalised the infliction, by an official holding a plurality of offices of a sentence passed by him in each capacity, but for the one offence.

"An unpretentious building ..."
The gate to the cell block at the infamous Port Arthur penal colony (1833) in Van Diemen's Land (now Tasmania). The photo was taken sometime between 1930 and 1950. The prison is now an Historic Site.

Annotations

1 **rough-hewn** (adj.): a piece of wood or stone that has been roughly cut and whose surface is not yet smooth – 2 **stockaded**: surrounded by a wall or fence made of large upright pieces of wood, built to defend a place or as in this case to keep prisoners inside – 4 **paneless aperture** (adj.): an opening or hole in a door or window without any sheet of glass – 6 **grate**: a frame of metal bars – **interstice** (n.): a small space or crack between things placed close together – 9 **hence**: into the future – 10 **stricken**: struck, hit – 12 **serge** (n.): strong, usually woollen cloth – 13 **hood**(v.): to put a hood over the prisoner's face for execution – 14 **to swinging the carcase**: hanging – 18 **VAN DIEMEN'S LAND** (n.): the former name (1642-1855) for Tasmania – 19 **convict** (n.): s.o. who has been proved to be guilty of a crime and sent to prison – **muster-station**: an area where the convicts must assemble (=gather, muster) to be assigned work duties – 24 **swell** (n.): (here) (old-fashioned for) a fashionable or important person – 26 **genial** (adj.): having a cheerful and friendly character or manner – 28 **goaded**: incited, pushed forward to do sth. – 31 **metalled roadway**: metal here means small stones for laying a road surface; – 38 **gubernatorial** (adj.): connected with the position of being a governor – **censured**: punished – 40 **duly-constituted**: appointed according to the law – 46 **penal servitude**: serving a prison (=penal) sentence – 47 **malediction** (n.): curse – 48 **benignant** (adj.): (false for) benign (= kind and gentle) – 50 **triangles**: a wooden structure with three sides on which men were tied and then whipped (=flogged) – 51 **gang-chains**: work gangs in chains, usu. chained ankle to ankle – **hominy** (n.): a food made from crushed sweet corn – **prodding**: pushing with a sharp object – 55 **capital doom**: execution, the death penalty ("capital" refers to original meaning of head, capital punishment is the common modern phrase) – 56 **gallows** (n., pl.): a structure used for killing criminals by hanging them from a rope – 57 **unflinching** (adj.): not changing or becoming weaker, even in a very difficult or dangerous situation – 59 **square** (n.): (here) a flat tool with a straight edge, often shaped like an L, used for drawing or measuring 90 degree angles – 60 **sturdy** (adj.): strong, well-made, not easily broken – 61 **cross-beam** (n.): a long heavy piece of wood or metal used in building houses, bridges etc. that spans from one support to another – 62 **plank** (n.): a long narrow, usu. heavy piece of wooden board, used especially for making structures to walk on – 63 **notched**: "notch" refers to a cut in a piece of wood or other material, enabling e.g. a rope to be held in place – 65 **rude**: rudimentary, simple, crude – 67 **droning**: talking in a boring way – 70 **morrow**: tomorrow, the

next day – 71 **garbed**: dressed, clothed – 72 **warder** (n.): s.o. who works in a prison guarding the prisoners – 73 **noosing the rope-end**: making a circle of the rope – 78 **iridescence** (n.): the display of colours that seem to change in different lights – 83 **quoth** (v.): (old use): (here) said – 87 **superintending**: looking after, looking over – 89 **PORT ARTHUR SETTLEMENT AND NORFOLK ISLAND**: two of the harshest places of punishment, actual places – 91 **embruted**: (an old word form) (here) his finer human feelings have been destroyed by the harshness of the convict system; he has become like a brute, a beast – 92 **eulogistic**: referring to s.th. or s.o. by using a lot of praise – 93 **wince** (v.): to suddenly change the expression on your face as a reaction to something painful or upsetting – 94 **depravity** (n.): the state or an instance of moral corruption – 95 **reprobate** (n.): a condemned, disreputable, or roguish person – 103 **sth. was amiss**: sth. had gone wrong – 103 **impetuously** (adv.): doing sth. very quickly, without thinking carefully first – 106 **musket** (n.): a type of gun used in former times – 107 **reverend functionary**: a clergyman who works as part of the government system – 113 **galled**: upset – 114 **fettered**: chained – 115 **eve**: the day before – 117 **infallibility**(n.): the principle or state of always being right and never making mistakes – 122 **conjectured**: guessed – 124 **unmanacled** (adj.): without chains on the hands/wrists; unchained – 125 **perpetrate**(v.): to do – 129 **sentinel** (n.): (old-fashioned term for) sentry (= a soldier standing outside a building as a guard) – **nodded**: fallen asleep – 130 **wrench** (n.): a twisting movement that pulls something violently – 131 **slumber** (n.): sleep – 132 **prise up** (v.): to insert sth. under an object to lift it; (here) using the bayonet to lift up a stone from the floor – **scoop out** (v.): (here) to pick sth. up with a bayonet – 134 **slipshod** (adj.): done too quickly and carelessly – 154 **scaling**: (here:) climbing to the top of the stockade – 156 **fracturing**: breaking, cracking – 158 **contumacious** (adj.): unreasonably disobedient – 159 **vexatious** (adj.): (old-fashioned) making you feel annoyed or worried – 160 **reposing**: resting – 164 **unprecedented** (adj.): never having happened before, or never having happened so much – 165 **minion**: a very unimportant person in an organization, who just obeys other people's orders – **groan** (v.): (here) to make a long deep sound because you are upset – 166 **abhorrent**: most hateful – 168 **to bolt** (v.): to escape – 169 **to be turned off**: (an unusual expression for) to be executed – **d-d**: damned – 171 **scragged**: (here) hanged, executed – 174 **to give legbail**: (here) run in order to escape from someone or something – 176 **noose** (n.): a ring formed by the end of a piece of rope or string, which closes more tightly as it is pulled – 177 **contrariness** (n.): (here) readiness to disagree or go against – 178 **innate**: natural – 180

craving (n.): an extremely strong desire for sth. – 181 **surged over**: became stronger than – 183 **crowning enormities**: his worst crimes – 184 **hubbub** (n.): a mixture of loud noises, especially the noise of a lot of people talking at the same time – 187 **regulars** (n., pl.): regulary military as well as the prison warders – 192 **whence** (adv.): (pronoun old use) from where – 196 **basil**: (here short form of "basilar") situated at the base of a bone of the skull, here: situated at the base of the ankle or anklet – 206 **hireling** (n.): s.o. who will work for anyone who is willing to pay – **hounds on their prey**: the dogs being hunted – 208 **sodger** (n.): (a dialect variant of) soldier – 211 **old cove**: (old, familiar term for) man, mate – 215 **desperado's**: s.o. who is desperate – 220 **lofty**: proud – 222 **jerk** (v.): to move with an irregular motion – 230 **lash** (n.): whip – 232 **cocoa** (n.): a sweet hot drink made with this powder, sugar, and milk or water – 238 **lashes**: (here) hits with the whip – 242 **By G**: By God – 247 **sneer** (v.): to smile or speak in a very unkind way that shows you have no respect for s.o. or s.th. – 251 **warrant** (n.): official paper authorising the punishment – 252 **cat-o'-nine** (n.): a whip with nine separate strands each with a knot at the end to increase the pain – 255 **to flay**: to strip the skin off – **stripes** (n., pl.): the strokes of the lash/whip – **pallet** (n.): (old-fashioned) a temporary bed, or a cloth bag filled with straw for sleeping on – 258 **yer**: used in writing as an infml. way of saying "you" – **sumthink**: (infml.) s.th. – **arden yer**: (infml.) (here) to harden your pain – 264 **coarse** (adj.): not fine, of inferior quality – 267 **apprised**: informed – 269 **javelin-men** (n..): (here) soldiers having rifles with bayonets – 281 **carrion** (n.): dead flesh that is decaying, (here) an ironic way of referring to the people who meet for the Coroner's Inquest – 283 **coroner** (n.): s.o. whose job is to discover the cause of s.o.'s death, esp. if they died in a sudden or unusual way – 284 **bethought** (v.) (past participle of "to bethink"): to remember sth. or think about sth. – 286 **sham** (adj.): made to appear real in order to deceive people; false

Questions

1   In the opening three paragraphs of the story how is Convict Glancy presented to us? How do you feel towards him in this early section of the story?

2   Why do you think the "Muster-Master" is given the name "Stoneman." Can you note any other names in the story which indicate something about a character or his official function?

3   As you were reading, did you feel sympathy for Convict Glancy despite his crimes? Can you describe how the story makes us feel sympathy towards this character?

4   As you are reading the story note examples of Warung's use of irony and his use of "official language." Try to describe how these examples influence they way we see the convict system, the officials, and the convict.

5   Check on a map for the location of Hobart and Port Arthur in Tasmania. Port Arthur was the main convict settlement in Tasmania. If your map is a good one you might also be able to find Oatlands, the township mentioned in the story.

Further reading: on the convict system, see Robert Hughes, *The Fatal Shore: A history of the transportation of convicts to Australia, 1787–1868.* Also visit the web sites for Port Arthur, Tasmania. Try: http://www.portarthur.org.au/convicts.htm.

Relics of convict discipline. Port Arthur, Tasmania.

RELICS OF CONVICT DISCIPLINE.   BEATTIE-HOBART.

2 | Henry Lawson

Henry Lawson (1867 – 1922) is Australia's best-known writer before the present period. He wrote poetry and short stories. Lawson was born on the goldfields at Grenfell, NSW. His father was from Norway; his name was Larsen, later changed to the more English form of Lawson. Lawson's early life was spent on the goldfields and on small farming properties in rural NSW (look for the towns of Mudgee, Gulgong and Eurunderee on a map; these names are all from the local Aboriginal language). His family was very poor. His mother, Louisa Lawson, left for Sydney where she later became an important writer and editor. Henry joined her in Sydney in 1883.

Lawson's first poems appeared in 1887 in Sydney newspapers. His first published story appeared in the *Bulletin* in 1888. He later travelled in outback NSW, Western Australia, Queensland, New Zealand, and England, but Sydney remained his base. His first collection of stories appeared in 1894 and his reputation was established by his second collection, *While the Billy Boils* (1896). He became Australia's most famous writer of the time, but his later life was unhappy. His marriage failed, he drank heavily and had money problems, and his writing suffered. Despite these difficulties he came to be seen by later readers as the first "truly Australian writer," especially for his stories of life in the Australian bush (the countryside). He was the first Australian writer to be given a State funeral, and he remains a "national icon." The critic A. G. Stephens wrote in 1895 that Lawson was "the voice of the bush, and the bush is the heart of Australia."

Lawson's reputation as the "voice of the bush" has sometimes prevented us seeing how complex his attitudes were. In this period, in the 1880s and 1890s, it was common for writers and artists to celebrate the Australian bush as a land of sunlight, freedom, wide, open spaces, and brave, hard-working pioneers. Because the Australian countryside was so distinctive, it had given to rise new ways of living and occupations. "The Drover's Wife" mentions droving and squatting (see Annotations). Many writers believed that the men and women of the bush represented the true Australians, a new type, formed by their new environment and therefore different from British people.

In some of his writings Lawson, too, expressed these views. But he was also aware of other aspects – that life in the bush could be lonely and frightening, especially for women; that the country could be hot, dangerous and cruel; that poverty and hardship were common. He knew this from his own experience. Both the positive and negative aspects are present in "The Drover's Wife" (1892). We can see the influence of "realism" on Lawson's writing, but perhaps he also creates a powerful "myth" of the Australian bush and its people.

This story is one of the best-known of all Australian stories. The figure of the woman alone is very memorable and moving, as she battles the snake, fire and flood, sickness, and strange men. She is isolated, except for her children, in a harsh, dreary land. The story shows her as just an ordinary woman, but it also gives her a certain heroic quality. Even if the environment is harsh, she now *belongs* there, more than anywhere else. She is "an Australian," as the story puts it. For many Australians, even today, the story seems to capture something unique about the Australian bush or outback.

THE DROVER'S WIFE

The two-roomed house is built of round timber, slabs, and stringy bark, and floored with split slabs. A big bark kitchen standing at one end is larger than the house itself, verandah included.

Bush all round – bush with no horizon, for the country is flat. No ranges in the distance. The bush consists of stunted, rotten native apple trees. No undergrowth. Nothing to relieve the eye save the darker green of a few sheoaks which are sighing above the narrow, almost waterless creek. Nineteen miles to the nearest sign of civilization – a shanty on the main road.

The drover, an ex-squatter, is away with sheep. His wife and children are left here alone.

Four ragged, dried-up-looking children are playing about the house. Suddenly one of them yells: "Snake! Mother, here's a snake!"

The gaunt, sun-browned bushwoman dashes from the kitchen, snatches her baby from the ground, holds it on her left hip, and reaches for a stick.

"Where is it?"

"Here! Gone into the wood-heap!" yells the eldest boy – a sharp-faced, excited urchin of eleven. "Stop there, mother! I'll have him. Stand back! I'll have the beggar!"

"Tommy, come here, or you'll be bit. Come here at once when I tell you, you little wretch!"

The youngster comes reluctantly, carrying a stick bigger than himself. Then he yells, triumphantly:

"There it goes – under the house!" and darts away with club up-lifted. At the same time the big, black, yellow-eyed dog-of-all breeds, who has shown the wildest interest in the proceedings, breaks his chain and rushes after that snake. He is a moment late, however, and his nose reaches the crack in the slabs just as the end of its tail disappears. Almost at the same moment the boy's club comes down and skins the aforesaid nose. Alligator takes small notice of this, and proceeds to undermine the building; but he is sub-dued after a struggle and chained up. They cannot afford to lose him.

The drover's wife makes the children stand together near the dog-house while she watches for the snake. She gets two small dishes of milk and sets them down near the wall to tempt it to come out; but an hour goes by and it does not show itself.

It is near sunset, and a thunderstorm is coming. The children must be brought inside. She will not take them into the house, for she knows the snake is there, and may at any moment come up

through the cracks in the rough slab floor; so she carries several armfuls of firewood into the kitchen, and then takes the children there. The kitchen has no floor – or, rather, an earthen one – called a
45 "ground floor" in this part of the bush. There is a large, roughly made table in the centre of the place. She brings the children in, and makes them get on this table. They are two boys and two girls – mere babies. She gives them some supper, and then, before it gets dark, she goes into the house, and snatches up some pillows and
50 bedclothes – expecting to see or lay her hand on the snake any minute. She makes a bed on the kitchen table for the children, and sits down beside it to watch all night.

She has an eye on the corner, and a green sapling club laid in readiness on the dresser by her side, together with her sewing bas-
55 ket and a copy of the *Young Ladies' Journal*. She has brought the dog into the room.

Tommy turns in, under protest, but says he'll lie awake all night and smash that blinded snake .

His mother asks him how many times she has told him not to
60 swear.

He has his club with him under the bedclothes, and Jacky protests:

"Mummy! Tommy's skinnin' me alive wif his club. Make him take it out."

65 Tommy: "Shet up, you little –! D'yer want to be bit with the snake?"

Jacky shuts up.

"If yer bit," says Tommy after a pause, "you'll swell up, an' smell, an' turn red an' green an' blue all over till yer bust. Won't he,
70 mother?"

"Now then, don't frighten the child. Go to sleep," she says.

The two younger children go to sleep, and now and then Jacky complains of being "skeezed". More room is made for him. Presently Tommy says: "Mother! listen to them (adjective) little 'pos-
75 sums. I'd like to screw their blanky necks."

And Jacky protests drowsily:

"But they don't hurt us, the little blanks!"

Mother: "There, I told you you'd teach Jacky to swear." But the remark makes her smile. Jacky goes to sleep.

80 Presently Tommy asks:

"Mother! Do you think they'll ever extricate the (adjective) kangaroo?"

"Lord! How am I to know, child? Go to sleep."

"Will you wake me if the snake comes out?"

"Yes. Go to sleep." 85

Near midnight. The children are all asleep and she sits there still, sewing and reading by turns. From time to time she glances round the floor and wall-plate, and whenever she hears a noise she reaches for the stick. The thunderstorm comes on, and the wind, rushing through the cracks in the slab wall, threatens to blow out her candle. 90 She places it on a sheltered part of the dresser and fixes up a newspaper to protect it. At every flash of lightning, the cracks between the slabs gleam like polished silver. The thunder rolls, and the rain comes down in torrents.

Alligator lies at full length on the floor, with his eyes turned to- 95 wards the partition. She knows by this that the snake is there. There are large cracks in that wall opening under the floor of the dwelling-house.

She is not a coward, but recent events have shaken her nerves. A little son of her brother-in-law was lately bitten by a snake, and 100 died. Besides, she has not heard from her husband for six months, and is anxious about him.

He was a drover, and started squatting here when they were married. The drought of 18 – ruined him. He had to sacrifice the remnant of his flock and go droving again. He intends to move his fa- 105 mily into the nearest town when he comes back, and, in the meantime, his brother, who keeps a shanty on the main road, comes over about once a month with provisions. The wife has still a couple of cows, one horse, and a few sheep. The brother-in-law kills one of the sheep occasionally, gives her what she needs of it, and takes the rest 110 in return for other provisions.

She is used to being left alone. She once lived like this for eighteen months. As a girl she built the usual castles in the air; but all her girlish hopes and aspirations have long been dead. She finds all the excitement and recreation she needs in the *Young Ladies' Journal,* 115 and, Heaven help her! takes a pleasure in the fashion-plates.

Her husband is an Australian, and so is she. He is careless, but a good enough husband. If he had the means he would take her to the city and keep her there like a princess. They are used to being apart, or at least she is. "No use fretting," she says. He may forget some- 120 times that he is married; but if he has a good cheque when he comes back he will give most of it to her. When he had money he took her to the city several times – hired a railway sleeping compartment, and put up at the best hotels. He also bought her a buggy, but they had to sacrifice that along with the rest. 125

The last two children were born in the bush – one while her husband was bringing a drunken doctor, by force, to attend to her. She

27

A bark-roof house (1868), the home of a pioneer family

was alone on this occasion, and very weak. She had been ill with a fever. She prayed to God to send her assistance. God sent Black Mary – the "whitest" gin in all the land. Or, at least, God sent "King Jimmy" first, and he sent Black Mary. He put his black face round the door-post, took in the situation at a glance, and said cheerfully. "All right, Missis – I bring my old woman, she down alonga creek."

One of her children died while she was here alone. She rode nineteen miles for assistance, carrying the dead child.

It must be near one or two o'clock. The fire is burning low. Alligator lies with his head resting on his paws, and watches the wall. He is not a very beautiful dog to look at and the light shows numerous old wounds where the hair will not grow. He is afraid of nothing on the face of the earth or under it. He will tackle a bullock as readily as he will tackle a flea. He hates all other dogs – except kangaroo-dogs – and has a marked dislike to friends or relations of the family. They seldom call, however. He sometimes makes friend with strangers. He hates snakes and has killed many, but he will be bitten some day and die; most snake-dogs end that way.

Now and then the bushwoman lays down her work and watches, and listens, and thinks. She thinks of things in her own life, for there is little else to think about.

The rain will make the grass grow, and this reminds her how she fought a bush fire once while her husband was away. The grass was long, and very dry, and the fire threatened to burn her out. She put on an old pair of her husband's trousers and beat out the flames with a green bough, till great drops of sooty perspiration stood out on her forehead and ran in streaks down her blackened arms. The sight of his mother in trousers greatly amused Tommy, who worked like a little hero by her side, but the terrified baby howled lustily for his "mummy". The fire would have mastered her but for four excited bushmen who arrived in the nick of time. It was a mixed-up affair all round; when she went to take up the baby he screamed and struggled convulsively, thinking it was a "black man"; and Alligator, trusting more to the child's sense than his own instinct, charged furiously, and (being old and slightly deaf) did not in his excitement at first recognize his mistress's voice, but continued to hang on to the moleskins until choked off by Tommy with a saddle-strap. The dog's sorrow for his blunder, and his anxiety to let it be known that it was all a mistake, was as evident as his ragged tail and a twelve-inch grin could make it. It was a glorious time for the boys; a day to look back to, and talk about, and laugh over for many years.

She thinks how she fought a flood during her husband's absence. She stood for hours in the drenching downpour, and dug an over-flow gutter to save the dam across the creek. But she could not save it. There are things that a bushwoman cannot do. Next morning the dam was broken, and her heart was nearly broken too, for she thought how her husband would feel when he came home and saw the result of years of labour swept away. She cried then.

She also fought the *pleuro-pneumonia* – dosed and bled the few re-maining cattle, and wept again when her two best cows died.

Again, she fought a mad bullock that besieged the house for a day. She made bullets and fired at him through cracks in the slabs with an old shotgun. He was dead in the morning. She skinned him and got seventeen-and-six for the hide.

She also fights the crows and eagles that have designs on her chickens. Her plan of campaign is very original. The children cry: "Crows, mother!" and she rushes out and aims a broomstick at the birds as though it were a gun, and says, "Bung!" The crows leave in a hurry; they are cunning, but a woman's cunning is greater.

Occasionally a bushman in the horrors, or a villainous-looking sundowner, comes and nearly scares the life out of her. She gener-ally tells the suspicious-looking stranger that her husband and two sons are at work below the dam, or over at the yard, for he always cunningly inquires for the boss.

Only last week a gallows-faced swagman – having satisfied him-self that there were no men on the place – threw his swag down on the verandah, and demanded tucker. She gave him something to eat; then he expressed his intention of staying for the night. It was sun-down then. She got a batten from the sofa, loosened the dog, and confronted the stranger, holding the batten in one hand and the dog's collar with the other. "Now you go!" she said. He looked at her and at the dog, said: "All right, mum," in a cringing tone, and left. She was a determined-looking woman and Alligator's yellow eyes glared unpleasantly – besides, the dog's chawing-up apparatus greatly resembled that of the reptile he was named after.

She has few pleasures to think of as she sits here alone by the fire, on guard against a snake. All days are much the same to her; but on Sunday afternoon she dresses herself, tidies the children, smartens up baby, and goes for a lonely walk along the bush-track, pushing an old perambulator in front of her. She does this every Sunday. She takes as much care to make herself and the children look smart as she would if she were going to do the block in the city. There is noth-ing to see, however, and not a soul to meet. You might walk for twenty miles along this track without being able to fix a point in your mind, unless you are a bushman. This is because of the ever-lasting, maddening sameness of the stunted trees – that monotony which makes a man to long break away and travel as far as trains can go, and sail as far as ships can sail – and further.   215

But this bushwoman is used to the loneliness of it. As a girl-wife she hated it, but now she would feel strange away from it.

She is glad when her husband returns, but she does not gush or make a fuss about it. She gets him something good to eat, and tidies up the children.   220

She seems contented with her lot. She loves her children, but has no time to show it. She seems harsh to them. Her surrounds are not favourable to the development of the "womanly" or sentimental side of nature.

It must be near morning now; but the clock is in the dwelling-house.   225
Her candle is nearly done; she forgot that she was out of candles. Some more wood must be got to keep the fire up, and so she shuts the dog inside and hurries round to the wood-heap. The rain has cleared off. She seizes a stick, pulls it out, and – crash! the whole pile collapses.   230

Yesterday she bargained with a stray blackfellow to bring her some wood, and while he was at work she went in search of a missing cow. She was absent an hour or so, and the native black made good use of his time. On her return she was so astonished to see a good heap of wood by the chimney, that she gave him an extra fig of   235
tobacco, and praised him for not being lazy. He thanked her, and left with head erect and chest well out. He was the last of his tribe and a King; but he had built that wood-heap hollow.

She is hurt now, and tears spring to her eyes as she sits down again by the table. She takes up a handkerchief to wipe the tears   240
away, but pokes her eyes with her bare fingers instead. The handkerchief is full of holes, and she finds that she has put her thumb through one, and her forefinger through another.

This makes her laugh, to the surprise of the dog. She has a keen, very keen, sense of the ridiculous; and some time or other she will   245
amuse bushmen with the story .

She has been amused before like that. One day she sat down "to have a good cry," as she said – and the old cat rubbed against her dress and "cried too." Then she had to laugh.

It must be near daylight. The room is very close and hot because of   250
the fire. Alligator still watches the wall from time to time. Suddenly he becomes greatly interested; he draws himself a few inches nearer

the partition, and a thrill runs through his body. The hair on the back of his neck begins to bristle, and the battle-light is in his yellow
255 eyes. She knows what this means, and lays her hand on the stick. The lower end of one of the partition slabs has a large crack on both sides. An evil pair of small, bright, bead-like eyes glisten at one of these holes. The snake – a black one – comes slowly out, about a foot, and moves its head up and down. The dog lies still, and the
260 woman sits as one fascinated. The snake comes out a foot further. She lifts her stick, and the reptile, as though suddenly aware of danger, sticks his head in through the crack on the other side of the slab, and hurries to get his tail round after him. Alligator springs, and his jaws come together with a snap. He misses, for his nose is large and
265 the snake's body down in the angle formed by the slabs and the floor. He snaps again as the tail comes round. He has the snake now, and tugs it out eighteen inches. Thud, thud comes the woman's club on the ground. Alligator pulls again. Thud, thud Alligator gives another pull and he has the snake out – a black brute, five feet long.
270 The head rises to dart about, but the dog has the enemy close to the neck. He is a big, heavy dog, but quick as a terrier. He shakes the snake as though he felt the original curse in common with mankind. The eldest boy wakes up, seizes his stick, and tries to get out of bed, but his mother forces him back with a grip of iron. Thud, thud – the
275 snake's back is broken in several places. Thud, thud – its head is crushed, and Alligator's nose skinned again.

She lifts the mangled reptile on the point of her stick, carries it to the fire, and throws it in; then piles on the wood, and watches the snake burn. The boy and dog watch, too. She lays her hand on the
280 dog's head, and all the fierce, angry light dies out of his yellow eyes. The younger children are quieted, and presently go to sleep. The dirty-legged boy stands for a moment in his shirt, watching the fire. Presently he looks up at her, sees the tears in her eyes, and, throwing his arms round her neck, exclaims:
285 "Mother, I won't never go drovin; blast me if I do!" And she hugs him to her worn-out breast and kisses him; and they sit thus together while the sickly daylight breaks over the bush.

Annotations

2 **slab** (n.): (here) a large timber panel cut roughly, a cheap building material in the Australian bush which can be made from local trees – **stringy bark**: a specific type of eucalyptus tree, in this context it refers to the bark of the stringy bark tree (it is not smooth bark but covered by rough string-like fibres) – 5 **stunted ... tree**: (here) a tree

that had been stopped from growing to its full size – 6 **undergrowth** (n.): the grasses and small bushes close to the ground – 7 **sheoak** (n.): (also: she-oak) any of various Australian trees of the genus *Casuarina*, having jointed leafless branches – 9 **shanty** (n.): a small, roughly built hut, cabin or house made from thin sheets of wood, tin, plastic etc. that poor people live in – 10 **drover** (n.): (in Australia) s.o. who "drives" cattle or sheep from one place to another, e.g. s.o. who accompanies a flock or group from one place to another on horseback; in Australia often over very long distances (hence he's away for long periods) – **ex-squatter** (n.): a person who used to live in an empty building or on a piece of land without permission and without paying rent; (here) a person who used to have land and his own sheep, but whose fortunes have declined in the meantime; the modern meaning of squatter implies poverty [in Australia "squatter" just meant s.o. who claims land, and in fact many of the 19th squatters became extremely wealthy] – 14 **gaunt** (adj.): (here) very thin and worn-out due to hard work in tough conditions – **dash** (v.): to move very quickly – 19 **urchin** (n.): (old-fashioned) a small dirty untidy child – 20 **beggar**: (here) nuisance – 22 **little wretch**: a naughty child – 25 **club** (n.): (here) a thick heavy stick used as a weapon to hit people or things – 31 **skin** (v.): (here) to hurt yourself or someone else by rubbing off some skin – 33 **undermine** (v.): to burrow underneath – 53 **sapling** (n.): a young tree – 58 **blinded**: (here) (infml.) bloody – 63 **Tommy's skinnin' me alive wif his club**: (sl.) "Tommy is skinning me alive with his club" (here: Jacky is complaining that Tommy took his club into bed with him and that this club is now rubbing skin off him) – 65 **shet up** (v.): (infml.) shut up; stop talking – **D'yer**: (here) used in writing as an infml. way of saying "Do you" – **bit with** (v.): the past tense of "bite" used with a wrong preposition; correct BrE usage: "bitten by" – 68 **yer bit**: (colloq.) you are bitten – **an'**: (colloq.) and – 69 **yer bust** (v.): you burst – 48 skeezed: squeezed in childish language – 74 **(adjective)**: narrative device of the author to suggest in a humorous way that the child uses a swear word; he puts "(adjective)" instead of a word like "bloody" (which was sometimes known as "the great Australian adjective") – **possum** (n.): one of various types of small furry animals that climb trees and live in America or Australia – 75 **blanky**: (infml.) bloody (cf. also footnote 49) – 77 **blanks**: (infml.) a more "polite" form of a swear word – 81 **extricate**: (infml.) childish misuse of the word "exterminate" – **(adjective)**: see footnote 74 – 94 **torrent** (n.): a large amount of water moving very rapidly and strongly in a particular direction; (here) heavy rain fall – 104 **drought** (n.): a long period of dry weather when there is not enough water for plants and animals to live – 105 **flock** (n.): (here) a group or herd of sheep – 116 **fashion-plates**: pictures of the latest fashion – 120 **fretting**: (esp. spoken English) to feel worried about small or unimportant things – 124 **buggy** (n.): (here) a two-wheeled horse-drawn carriage – 129 **Black Mary**: an Aboriginal woman – 130 **the "whitest"**: "white" is used here to signify goodness and virtue, a common usage at this time; so the "irony" is that the black woman is "white" in this sense – **gin**: (here) (infml.) an offensive term for "Aboriginal female" – **King Jimmy**: (infml.) an Aboriginal man; white settlers would often give Aborigines a name like "King," esp. to the elders or leaders of a local group or tribe – 133 **she down alona creek**: (colloq.) she is down at the "creek" (= AustrE; a small narrow stream or river) – 140 **bullock** (n.): a young male cow that cannot breed – 141 **kangaroo-dogs** (n., pl.): dogs bred for hunting kangaroos – 153 **bough** (n.): a main branch on a tree – 158 **in the nick of time**: just before it is too late or just before sth. bad happens – 160 **convulsively**: with violent, uncontrolled movements – 164 **moleskin** (n.): (here) trousers made from a heavy material; work trousers – 165 **blunder** (n.): a careless or stupid mistake – 170 **drenching downpour:** lot of rain that falls in a short time and makes everything extremely wet – 176 **pleuro-pneu-monia:** (BrE "pleurisy") (here) a serious illness which affects cattle, esp. the lungs, causing severe pain in the chest making it difficult to breathe – 181 **hide**: (here) his skin; the leather – 186 **cunning**: clever, resourceful – 187 **the horrors**: a term used to describe the effects sometimes produced in men who had to spend long periods alone in the bush, sometimes close to madness; sometimes also used to re-fer to men suffering from too much alcohol – **villainous**: evil – 188 **sundowner** (n.): s.o. like a swagman, an itinerant worker, or beggar; so-called because he turns up at your house at sun down asking for food and/or lodging – 192 **gallows-faced**: mean-looking – **swagman** (n.): (AustrE) s.o. who travels on foot and carries a set of clothes and possessions wrapped in a cloth – 194 **tucker** (n.): (AustrE, NZE) (infml.) food – 196 **batten** (n.): a narrow piece of wood – 207 **peram-bulator** (n.): (old-fashioned esp. BrE) a pram – 209 **do the block in the city**: "the block" was the most fashionable part of the city where people would dress in their best and "promenade" – 218 **gush** (v.): to express one's emotions very strongly – 225 **dwelling-house** (n.): a house that people live in, not one that is being used as a shop, office etc. – 231 **blackfellow** (n.): Aborigine – 235 **fig**: amount, ration – 250 **close**: (here) of a warm atmosphere, stifling – 254 **bristle** (v.): to stand up straight – 285 **I won't … drovin'**: (infml.) I won't ever go droving – **blast me if I do**: (infml.) I'll be damned if I do.

Questions

1   Note carefully the way Lawson describes the house and surrounding land. What are the key words in creating this picture of the bush? Note the format of his sentences – short and to the point (e.g. "No undergrowth"). What effect do you think this way of writing creates?

2   How are the wife and children described early in the story?

3   Notice that most of the story is told in the present tense rather than the past tense used by most story writers. Try to write some comments about how this technique helps create the atmosphere of the story. Also, as you are reading through the story, note those sections where it moves to the past tense (e.g, when she fights the bush fire). How does the structure help create the story's effects?

4   The "wife" is given no name. Why do you think Lawson chose to write the story this way – drawing attention to this character by the story's title but then not giving her an individual name?

5   An Australian painter, Russel Drysdale, painted a famous painting in 1945 also called "The Drover's Wife." Try to find a reproduction of this painting (perhaps in your library or try searching the web site of the Australian National Gallery [http://www.nga.gov.au/Home/index.cfm] which sometimes shows this painting). If you can view it, compare the image with your impressions of Lawson's story – do you think Drysdale has been influenced by Lawson's story? Does the painting match your impressions of the story?

6   Think about the story's ending: what is suggested by the boy's cry to his mother, and the final image of the "sickly daylight"?

For further reading, try to find more of Lawson's stories. Some recommended stories are: "In a Wet Season" and "In a Dry Season," "The Union Buries Its Dead," "Rats" and "Water them Geraniums." You might also like to compare with a female perspective by reading stories by Barbara Baynton. Her collection is called *Bush Stories*; one of her most famous stories is "The Chosen Vessel."

3 | Thea Astley

Thea Astley was born in Brisbane in 1925. She was educated at the University of Queensland and was a school teacher and a university lecturer (at Macquarie University, NSW, 1968 – 80). Her first novel was published in 1958, and by 2002 she had published 13 novels and 3 books of short stories. She has also won many awards and prizes, including the Miles Franklin Award, Australia's most important prize for a novel, on four occasions, in 1962, 1965, 1972 and 2000.

Astley's fiction often deals with outsiders or "misfits," those who don't quite fit into the normal patterns of Australian life. Many of her works are set in Northern Queensland, where the tropical climate and environment often seem to match the exaggerated or unusual behaviour of her characters. She can write about Australian society with bitter satire, criticising complacent or pretentious attitudes.

Astley was among a group of women writers who rose to prominence in Australia in the 1970s and 1980s (although she began publishing much earlier). This new wave of women's writing was one of the most important developments in Australian literature in this period, challenging the emphasis on male writers and men's experience which had been predominant for much of the previous century. Although Astley does not necessarily take an overt feminist position, she is extremely sensitive to the female perspective in her stories.

This is certainly the case in "Heart is Where the Home Is." The two main characters are women, Nelly, the young Aboriginal mother, and Mag Laffey, the white farm woman. Although the story asks us to think deeply about issues of racial inequality as suffered by the Aborigines in Australia, it also suggests that there are bonds between these two characters as women and mothers.

Astley's story is remarkable because of the way she uses Aboriginal English – imitating the patterns of common forms of Aboriginal speech – in order to represent Nelly's thoughts and feelings as well as her speech. Astley does not specify the time at which the story is set – one can guess some time in the mid-twentieth century – but the government policies she refers to were practised in Australia from the nineteenth century through to the 1950s.

Governments in the Australian States introduced policies for the removal of Aboriginal children from their families. These policies applied especially to children of mixed Aboriginal-white parents, who were to be removed from Aboriginal communities and placed in institutions, run by government or church organisations. They would be educated in white ways and then they could assimilate into white society.

It is true that conditions in Aboriginal camps and households were often poor. But as the story shows powerfully, the bond between "heart" and "home" is extremely powerful. While the official justification was that removal was "for the child's own good," Aboriginal mothers suffered terribly, families were broken, and the children experienced the problems common to children worldwide who grow up in institutions. Very few were educated in the same way as white people. These past practices have recently become one of the most important issues in Australia. In 1997, a large Report (called *Bringing them Home*) was released which recorded the experiences of those now known as the "Stolen Generation." Australians are still coming to terms with the pain and suffering caused to Aboriginal families and children.

Astley's story recreates the conflict between the official white world and the human world of the Aboriginal people. While Mag Laffey's feelings of natural justice lead her to defend Nelly, the story also shows how even the sympathetic white, George, cannot fully understand Nelly's sense of "home."

HEART IS WHERE THE HOME IS

The morning the men came, policemen, someone from the government, to take the children away from the black camp up along the
river, first there was the wordless terror of heart-jump, then the
wailing, the women scattering and trying to run dragging their kids,
5 the men sullen, powerless before this new white law they'd never
heard of. Even the coppers felt lousy seeing all those yowling gins.
They'd have liked the boongs to show a bit of fight, really, then they
could have laid about feeling justified.

But no. The buggers just took it. Took it and took it.
10 The passivity finally stuck in their guts.

Bidgi Mumbler's daughter-in-law grabbed her little boy and fled
through the scrub patch towards the river. Her skinny legs didn't
seem to move fast enough across that world of the policeman's eye.
She knew what was going to happen. It had happened just the week
15 before at a camp near Tobaccotown. Her cousin Ruthie lost a kid that
way.

"We'll bring her up real good," they'd told Ruthie. "Take her
away to big school and teach her proper, eh? You like your kid to
grow up proper and know about Jesus?"
20 Ruthie had been slammed into speechlessness.

Who were they?

She didn't understand. She knew only this was her little girl.
There was all them words, too many of them, and then the hands.

There had been a fearful tug-o'-war; the mother clinging to the
25 little girl, the little girl clutching her mother's dress, and the welfare
officer with the police, all pulling, the kid howling, the other
mothers egg-eyed, gripping their own kids, petrified, no men
around, the men tricked out of camp.

Ruthie could only whimper, but then, as the policeman started to
30 drag her child away to the buggy, she began a screeching that
opened up the sky and pulled it down on her.

She bin chase that buggy two miles till one of the police he ride
back on his horse an shout at her an when she wouldn't take no notice she bin run run run an he gallop after her an hit her one two,
35 cracka cracka, with his big whip right across the face so the pain get
all muddle with the cryin and she run into the trees beside the track
where he couldn follow. She kep goin after that buggy, fightin her
way through scrub but it wasn't no good. They too fast. An then the
train it come down the line from Tobaccotown an that was the last
40 she see her little girl, two black legs an arms, strugglin as the big
white man he lift her into carriage from the sidin.

"You'll have other baby," Nelly Mumbler comforted her. "You'll have other baby." But Ruthie kept sittin, wouldn do nothin. Jus sit an rock an cry an none of the other women they couldn help, their kids gone too and the men so angry they jus drank when they could get it an their rage burn like scrub fire.

Everything gone: Land. Hunting grounds. River. Fish. Gone. New god come. Old talk still about killings. The old ones remembering the killings.

"Now they take our kids," Jackie Mumbler said to his father, Bidgi. "We make kids for whites now. Can't they make their own kids, eh? Take everythin. Land. Kids. Don't give nothin, only take."

So Nelly had known the minute she saw them whites comin down the track. The other women got scared, fixed to the spot like they grow there, all shakin and whimperin. Stuck. "You'll be trouble," they warned. "You'll be trouble."

"Don't care," she said. "They not takin my kid."

She wormed her way into the thickest part of the rain forest, following the river, well away from the track up near the packers' road. Her baby held tightly against her chest, she stumbled through vine and over root, slashed by leaves and thorns, her eyes wide with fright, the baby crying in little gulps, nuzzling in at her straining body.

There'd bin other time year before she still hear talk about. All them livin up near Tinwon. The govmin said for them all to come long train. Big surprise, eh, an they all gone thinkin tobacco, tucker, blankets. An the men, they got all the men out early that day help work haulin trees up that loggin camp and the women they all excited waitin long that train, all the kids playin, and then them two policemen they come an start grabbin, grabbin all the kids, every kid, and the kids they screamin an the women they all cryin an tuggin an some, they hittin themselves with little sticks. One of the police, he got real angry and start shovin the women back hard. He push an push an then the train pulls out while they pushin an they can see the kids clutchin at the windows and some big white woman inside that train, she pull them back.

Nelly dodged through wait-a-while, stinging-bush, still hearing the yells of the women back at the camp. Panting and gasping, she came down to the water where a sand strip ran half way across the river. If she crossed she would only leave tracks. There was no time to scrape away telltale footprints. She crept back into the rain forest and stood trembling, squeezing her baby tightly, trying to smother his howls, but the baby wouldn't hush, so she huddled under a bush and comforted him with her nipples for a while, his round eyes staring up at her as he sucked while she regained her breath.

85   Shouts wound through the forest like vines.

Wailing filtered through the canopy.

Suddenly a dog yelped, too close. She pulled herself to her feet, the baby still suckling, and went staggering along the sandy track by the riverbank, pushing her bony body hard, thrusting between claws of 90 branch and thorn, a half mile, a mile, until she knew that soon the forest cover would finish and she'd be out on the fence-line of George Laffey's place, the farm old Bidgi Mumbler had come up and worked for. She'd been there, too, now and then, help washin, cleanin, when young Missus Laffey makin all them pickles an things.

95   For a moment she stood uncertain by the fence, then on impulse she thrust her baby under the wire and wriggled through after him, smelling the grass, smelling ants, dirt, all those living things, and then she grabbed him up and stumbled through the cow paddock down to the mango trees, down past the hen yard, the vegetable 100 garden, down over a lawn with flower-blaze and the felty shadows of tulip trees, past Mister Laffey spading away, not stopping when he looked up at her, startled, but gasping past him round the side of the house to the back steps and the door that was always open.

Mag Laffey came to the doorway and the two young women 105 watched each other in a racket of insect noise. A baby was crying in a back room and a small girl kept tugging at her mother's skirts.

The missus was talkin, soft and fast. Nelly couldn't hear nothin and then hands, they pull her in, gently, gently, but she too frightened hanging onto Charley, not lettin go till the white missus she 110 put them hands on her shoulders and press her down onto one them kitchen chairs an hold her. "Still, now," her voice keep sayin. "Still."

So she keep real still and the pretty white missus say, "Tell me, Nelly. You tell me what's the matter."

115   It took a while, the telling, between the snuffles and the coaxing and the gulps and swallowed horrors.

"I see," Mag Laffey said at last. "I see," she said again, her lips tightening. "Oh I see."

She eased the baby from Nelly's arms and put him down on the 120 floor with her own little girl, watching with a smile as the children stared then reached out to touch each other. She went over to the stove and filled the teapot and handed the black girl a cup, saying, "You drink that right up now and then we'll think of something. George will think of something."

125   It was half an hour before the policemen came. They rode down the track from the railway line at an aggressive trot, coming to halt beside George as he rested on his spade.

Confronted with their questions he went blank. "Only the house-girl." And added, "And Mag and the kids."

The police kicked their horses on through his words and George slammed his spade hard into the turned soil and followed them down to where they were tethering their horses at the stair rails. He could see them boot-thumping up the steps. The house lay open as a palm.

Mag forestalled them, coming out onto the verandah. Her whole body was a challenge.

"Well," she asked, "what is it?" The big men fidgeted. They'd had brushes with George Laffey's wife before, so deceptively young and pliable, a woman who never knew her place, always airing an idea of some sort. Not knowing George's delight with her, they felt sorry for that poor bastard of a husband who'd come rollicking home a few years back from a trip down south with a town girl with town notions.

"Government orders, missus," one said. "We have to pick up all the abo kids. All abo kids have got to be taken to special training schools. It's orders."

Mag Laffey inspected their over-earnest faces. She couldn't help smiling.

"Are you asking me, sergeant, if I have any half-caste children, or do I misunderstand?" She could hardly wait for their reaction.

The sergeant bit his lower lip and appeared to chew something before he could answer. "Not you personally, missus." Disgusting, he thought, disgusting piece of goods, making suggestions like that. "We just want to know if you have any round the place? Any belonging to that lot up at the camp?"

"Why would I do that?"

"I don't know, missus." He went stolid. "You've got a housegirl, haven't you? Your husband said."

"Yes, I do."

"Well then, has she got any kids?"

"Not that I am aware of," Mag Laffey lied vigorously. Her eyes met theirs with amused candour.

"Maybe so. But we'd like to speak to her. You know it's breaking the law to conceal this."

"Certainly I know." George was standing behind the men at the foot of the steps, his face nodding her on. "You're wasting your time here let me tell you. You're wasting mine as well. But that's what government's for, isn't it?"

"I don't know what you mean, missus." His persistence moved him forward a step. "Can we see that girl or not?"

Mag called over her shoulder down the hall but stood her ground at the doorway, listening to Nelly shuffle, unwilling, along the lino. When she came up to the men, she still had a dishcloth in her hands that dripped suds onto the floor. Her eyes would not meet those of
175 the big men blocking the light.

"Where's your kid, Mary?" the sergeant asked, bullying and jocular. "You hiding your kid?"

Nelly dropped her head and shook it dumbly.

"Cat got your tongue?" the other man said. "You not wantem
180 talk, eh? You lying?"

"She has no children," Mag Laffey interrupted coldly. "I told you that. Perhaps the cat has your ears as well. If you shout and nag and humiliate her, you'll never get an answer. Can't you understand something as basic as that? You're frightening her."
185 She looked past the two of them at her husband who was smiling his support.

"Listen, lady," the sergeant said, his face congested with the suppressed need to punch this cheeky sheilah right down her own hallway, "that's not what they tell me at the camp."
190 "What's not what they tell you?"

"She's got a kid all right. She's hiding it some place."

George's eyes, she saw, were strained with affection and concern. Come up, her own eyes begged him. Come up. "Sergeant," she said, "I have known Nelly since she was a young girl. She's helped out
195 here for the last four years. Do you think I wouldn't know if she had a child? Do you? But you're free to search the house, if you want, and the grounds. You're thirsting for it, aren't you, warrant or not?"

The men shoved roughly past her at that, flattening Nelly Mumbler against the wall, and creaked down the hallway, into bedrooms
200 and parlor and out into the kitchen. Cupboard doors crashed open. There was a banging of washhouse door.

George came up the steps and took his wife's arm, steering her and Nelly to the back of the house and putting them behind him as he watched the police come in from the yard.
205 "Satisfied?"

"No, we're not, mate," the sergeant replied nastily. "Not one bloody bit."

Their powerful bodies crowded the kitchen out. They watched contemptuously as Nelly crept back to the sink, her body tensed
210 with fright.

"We don't believe you, missus," the sergeant said. "Not you or your hubby. There'll be real trouble for both of you when we catch you out."

Mother and child at an Aborigine outstation

Mag held herself braced against infant squawls that might expose them at any minute. She made herself busy stoking the stove.

"Righto," George said, pressing her arm and looking sharp and hard at the other men. "You've had your look. Now would you mind leaving. We've all got work to get on with."

The sergeant was sulky. He scraped his boots about and kept glancing around the kitchen and out the door into the back garden. The Laffeys' small girl was getting under his feet and pulling at his trouser legs, driving him crazy.

"All right," he agreed reluctantly. "All right." He gave one last stare at Nelly's back. "Fuckin' boongs," he said, deliberately trying to offend that stuck-up Mrs Laffey. "More trouble than they're worth. And that's bloody nothing."

The two women remained rooted in the kitchen while George went back up the track to his spadework. The sound of the horses died away.

At the sink Nelly kept washing and washing, her eyes never leaving the suds, the dishmop, the plate she endlessly scoured. Even after the thud of hoof faded beyond the ridge, even after that. And even after Mag Laffey took a cloth and began wiping the dishes and stacking them in the cupboard, even after that.

Mag saw her husband come round the side of the house, toss his hat on an outside peg and sit on the top step to ease his earth-stuck clobbers of boots off. Nelly's stiffly curved back asked question upon question. Her long brown fingers asked. Her turned-away face asked. When her baby toddled back into the kitchen, taken down from the bedroom ceiling manhole where George had hidden him with a lolly to suck, Nelly stayed glued to that sink washing that one plate.

"Come on, Nelly," Mag said softly. "What's the matter? We've beaten them, haven't we?"

George had picked up the small black boy and his daughter and was bouncing a child on each knee, waggling his head lovingly between them both while small hands pawed his face.

Infinitely slowly, Nelly turned from the sink, her fingers dripping soap and water. She looked at George Laffey cuddling a white baby and a black but she couldn't smile. "Come nex time," she said, hopeless. "Come nex time."

George and his wife looked at her with terrible pity. They knew this as well. They knew.

"And we'll do the same next time," Mag Laffey stated. "You don't have to worry."

Then George Laffey said, "You come live here, Nelly. You come all time, eh?" His wife nodded at each word. Nodded and smiled and cried a bit. "You and Charley, eh?"

Nelly opened her mouth and wailed. *What is it?* they kept asking. *What's the matter? Wouldn't you like that?* They told her she could 260 have the old store shed down by the river. They'd put a stove in and make it proper. Nelly kept crying, her dark eyes an unending fountain, and at last George became exasperated.

"You've got no choice, Nelly," he said, dropping the baby pidgin he had never liked anyway. "You've got no choice. If you come here 265 we can keep an eye on Charley. If you don't, the government men will take him away. You don't want that, do you? Why don't you want to come?"

"Don't want to leave my family," she sobbed. "Don't want." "God love us," George cried from the depths of his non-understanding, 270 "God love us, they're only a mile up the river." He could feel his wife's fingers warning on his arm. "You can see them whenever you want."

"It's not same," Nelly insisted and sobbed. "Not same." George thought he understood. He said, "You want Jackie, then. You want 275 your husband to come along too, work in the garden maybe? Is that it?"

He put the baby into her arms and the two of them rocked somberly before him. He still hadn't understood.

The old men old women uncles aunts cousins brothers sisters tin 280 humpies bottles dogs dirty blankets tobacco handouts fights river trees all the tribe's remnants and wretchedness, destruction and misery.

Her second skin now.

"Not same," she whispered. And she cried them centuries of tri- 285 bal dream in those two words. "Not same."

Annotations

4 **wailing**: crying out with a long, high sound, esp. because you are very sad or in pain; **weeping and wailing:** weeping and wailing with grief – 5 **sullen** (adj.): silently showing anger or bad temper – 6 **copper** (n.): (in BrE infml. for) "police officer" – **yowling gins**: (infml.) (derog.) Aboriginal women who utter long, distressful or dismal cries; "gin" is an offensive word for an Aboriginal woman – 7 **boong** (n.): (AustrE) (offensive) a coloured person – 10 **the passivity finally stuck in their guts**: eventually the passivity of the Aborigines caused them (= the police) to feel resentment, frustration and anger – 12 **patch** (n.): (here) a small piece, a small area of land – 18

teach her proper: (sl.) teach her properly/correctly – 23 **all them words**: (sl.) all those words – 24 **tug-o'-war**: (tug of war) (here) a hard struggle between two equally matched factions – 25 **clutch**: to hold sth. or s.o. tightly, esp. because you are frightened, in pain, or do not want to lose sth. – 27 **egg-eyed**: (a poetic image) eyes as big as eggs – **petrified** (adj.): extremely frightened, especially so frightened that you cannot move or think – 30 **buggy**: a two-wheeled horse-drawn carriage – 34 **she bin run run run an**: she has been running for a very long time and – 35 **cracka cracka**: (infml.) word formation to articulate a sudden sharp noise caused by a whip and its intensity – 36 **cryin**: (infml.) crying – 37 **couldn**: (infml.) couldn't – **kep goin**: (infml.) kept going – **fightin**: (infml.) fighting – 38 **wasn't no good**: (Abor.) (double negation is a typical element in Aboriginal and other pidgin or Kriol languages which have a simple grammatical structure), (here) wasn't of any good, it didn't help – 39 **an**: (infml.) and – 40 **strugglin**: (infml.) struggling – 41 **sidin**: (infml.) siding (= a rail line that goes off the main rail line where they park trains or carriages, or a short branch track used for shunting, or loading a rail); (here) the big white man was next to the carriage on the siding, or even at the small platform or raised area of earth next to the siding from which things can be loaded – 43 **other**: (infml.) another – **sittin ... fire**: (infml.) sitting and wouldn't do anything. She just sat in her place and cried and none of the other women could help as their kids had been taken, too, and the men were so angry that they just drank when they couldn't bear it any more and their rage was burning like scrub fire – 52 **Take everythin**: (infml.) They take everything – **don't give nothin'**: (Abor.) (infml.) They don't give anything (to us) – 53 **them whites comin**: (Abor.) (infml.) the whites coming – 55 **all shakin and whimperin**: (infml.): shaking and whimpering all over – **you'll be trouble**: (infml.) you will be in trouble – 57 **don't ... kid**: (infml.) I don't care ... They are not taking ... – 63 **There'd bin ... talk about**: (infml.) (Colloq. English would use here "There had been another time a year before and she still hears people talking about it") People still talk about a similar event that had happened a year before – **all them ... blankets**: (infml.) All of them were living up there near Tinwon. The government told them to get on a long train. It was a big surprise, eh, and they all went thinking about tobacco, tucker, blankets – 64 **govmin**: (sl.) government – 65 **tucker** (n.): (AustrE) food – 65/68 **long**: (Abor.) "long" has a very distinctive meaning in Aboriginal languages and Pidgin and illustrates the influence of BrE on these languages particularly in the 19th c.; it supposedly originates in (BrE) "come along" meaning "come here" or "follow me" – **to come long train**: (Abor.) go to the train – 66 **An ...**

little sticks: And the men, they got all the men out early that day to help with the work, hauling [pulling] ... the women were all excited waiting along the train and all the kids were playing there. And then two policemen came and started grabbing, ... the kids were screaming and the women were all crying and tugging (to tug: to pull with one or more short, quick pulls) and some were hitting themselves with little sticks – 67 **loggin**: (Abor.) (logging) i.e. timber gathering, tree felling – 68 **waitin long that train**: (Abor.) (waiting' long that train) waiting for that train to come; (here) "long" is just used to emphasize that they were there – 71 **One ...back**: One of the policemen got really angry and started shoving the women back hard. He pushed and pushed and then the train pulled out while they were pushing. And they could see the kids clutching at the ... train pulled them back – 76 **dodge** (v.): to move quickly in order to avoid being hit by someone or something – 77 **panting**: breathing quickly with short noisy breaths because you have been running, climbing etc or because it is very hot – **gasping**: breathing quickly and deeply because you are having difficulty getting air – 86 **canopy** (n.): the uppermost growth on trees in a rainforest – 98 **paddock** (n.): (AustrE, NZE) a field, esp. one with grass – 101 **tulip trees** (n.): any of various trees with tulip-shaped flowers, such as the magnolia – 107 **missus** (n.): (infml.) a man's wife; (here) "missus" refers esp. to the owner's wife (particularly Aboriginal towards white) – **talkin**: (infml.) talking – **nothin**: (infml.) nothing – **then ... in**: (infml.) then the hands pulled her in – 108 **but ... Charley**: (infml.) but she was too frightened hanging on to Charley – 109 **lettin**: (infml.) letting – **she put ... her**: (infml.) she put her hands on her shoulders and pressed her down on to one of the kitchen chairs and held her – 111 **keep sayin**: (infml.) kept saying – 113 **keep:** kept very still – 115 **coaxing**(n): persuasion – 127 **spade** (n.): a tool for digging that has a long handle and a broad metal blade you push into the ground – 132 **tether**: to tie an animal with a rope or chain so that it can only move around within a limited area – 134 **palm** (n.): (here) referring to the hand, "the palm" of an open hand – 135 **forestall** (v.): to prevent sth. from happening or prevent s.o. from doing sth. by doing sth. first – 137 **fidget** (v.): to keep moving – 139 **pliable** (adj.): (here) easily influenced – 141 **rollicking**: noisy and cheerful – 145 **abo**: (short for) Aboriginal – 149 **half-caste** (adj.): having parents who are of different races; word is now considered offensive – 153 **disgusting piece of goods**: (derog.) an offensive way to refer to the woman like some merchandise – 157 **stolid** (adj.): impassive – 162 **candour** (n.): sincere honesty and truthfulness – 172 **shuffle**: walking slowly without lifting your feet of the ground – **lino**: (infml.) linoleum (= a particular floor covering) – 176 **jocular** (adj.): joking or humorous – 179 **Cat got your tongue? ... You not wantem talk**: (infml.) "You don't want to talk;" a common saying esp. to children when they don't want to talk – 180 **You lying**: (infml.) You are lying – 187 **congested** (adj.): crowded, (here) almost like a face about to explode – 188 **sheilah**: (AustrE or NZE slang) a young woman – 197 **warrant**: (here) an authorisation to search private premises, e.g. police can't enter a private house etc. without obtaining authorisation (= a warrant) from a government official – 200 **parlour** (n.): (old-fashioned) a room in a house which has comfortable chairs and is used for meeting guests – 215 **stoking**: adding more coal or wood to a fire used for cooking or heating – 219 **sulky** (adj.): showing that you are annoyed about sth. by being silent and having an unhappy expression on your face – 231 **to scour** (v.): (here) to wash the plate by rubbing it vigorously with a cloth, esp. one with a rough surface – 236 **peg** (n.): a short piece of wood, metal etc. fixed to a wall or door, used for hanging things on, esp. clothes – 237 **clobber** (n.): (here) big heavy boots – 251 **come nex time**: (infml.) They will return – 256 **You come live ... time**: (infml.) You can stay with us permanently – 269 **God love us**: (here) Good heavens! or Heavens above!; an exclamation with a slight note of despair and frustration here – 281 **humpy** (n.): (AustrE) a primitive hut, esp. used to refer to Aboriginal dwellings – 285 **not same**: not the same

Questions

1 In English there is a common saying that "home is where the heart is." Astley changes the places of the words "home" and "heart" in her title. Why do you think she does that? What meaning does her title carry (try to relate it to the events of the story)?

2 You can read some of the Report on the Stolen Generation by going to the web site of the Australian *Human Rights and Equal Opportunity Commission* at http://www.hreoc.gov.au/ Follow the links from *Aboriginal and Torres Strait Islander Social Justice* to *Stolen Children.*

3 How are the authorities, the policeman, shown in this story?

4 Try to describe in your own words Nelly's feelings for her home. How is it different from George's understanding?

4 | David Malouf

David Malouf is one of Australia's most successful contemporary writers. He has won many awards in Australia and internationally, and his books have been translated into many languages. David Malouf was born in Brisbane in 1934. His father's family came to Australia in the 1880s from Lebanon, and his mother's family from England some time later. He writes about his childhood in *12 Edmondstone Street* (1985). He was educated at the University of Queensland and taught there for some time. He then left for England and Europe. In 1968 he returned to Australia to work at the University of Sydney. He spent many years living half in Sydney and half in Tuscany, Italy.

Malouf has written 6 novels, 3 books of short stories, 2 books of novellas (a novella is a long short story), and several books of poetry. As well as winning many prizes in Australia, he has been awarded the Neustadt International Prize for Literature (2000), the Lannan Literary Award (USA), the International Dublin Literary Award, Prix Baudelaire (France), *Los Angeles Times* Book Prize, and Commonwealth Writers' Prize among other international literary awards. His best-known novels are *Remembering Babylon* (1993), *The Great World* (1990), *An Imaginary Life* (1978), all of which have been translated into German, and *Johnno* (1975), his first novel.

Perhaps the most common theme in Malouf's novels and short stories is the idea of "place." He writes about rooms, houses, landscapes, cities, regions, and even Australia as a nation. He explores our feelings of belonging to certain places, our deep emotional attachment to places, the connections between our sense of identity and certain places in nature or in the human environment. In particular, he explores the role of our imagination – how our thoughts, feelings, dreams and fears might be shaped by our relationship with the natural or social world around us.

Perhaps coming from a migrant family Malouf is especially sensitive to these questions. Possibly also growing up in Brisbane, Queensland, has made him interested in this theme, too, because until the 1980s Brisbane was a small city compared to Sydney and Melbourne. Thus, he is concerned with questions like: What did it mean to grow up in Brisbane? How was that different from growing up in Sydney or Melbourne – or London or another major international city? Finally, Malouf's exploration of this theme leads him to reflect on what it means to be Australian too – can Australians who are not Aborigines ever really feel they belong to this land? Or must they remain settlers, colonials, in someone else's land?

These final questions are explored in "Blacksoil Country" which first appeared in the collection *Dream Stuff* (2000). The story is told in the voice of the young boy, Jordan McGivern, whose family has moved onto this land (sometime in the 19th century) as farmers. The original owners, the Aborigines, are still living in the area, and the boy's father is determined to keep them off "his land" (for them, of course, it is still their land). The father's attitude is contrasted to that of their neighbour, Mick Jolley.

As well as the story of the boy's relationship with his father and his father's relationship with the Aborigines, with its tragic results, the story also presents us with different feelings about the land. Jordan loves it; he calls it "my sort of country." He explores it, and finds it full of life, full of voices, even "ghosts." He does not feel threatened by the Aborigines. His father's attitudes are very different.

The story reaches an inevitable climax when the father shoots one of the Aborigines. But then the story takes an unusual turn. It appears that the boy disappears into the bush and is killed by the Aborigines. His father becomes a local hero seeking revenge against the local Aborigines for the loss of his son. But although the boy is dead, it is still his voice which is telling the story to us.

BLACKSOIL COUNTRY

This is blacksoil country. Open, empty, crowded with ghosts, figures
hidden away in the folds of it who are there, who are here, even if
they are not visible and no one knows it but a few who look up suddenly into a blaze of sunlight and feel the hair crawl on their neck
and know they are not the only ones. That they are being watched or
tracked. They'll go on then with a sense for a moment that their
body, as it goes, leaves no dent in the air.

Jordan my name is. Jordan McGivern. I am twelve years old. I can
show you this country. I been in it long enough.

When we first come up here, Pa and Ma and Jamie and me, we
were the first ones on this bit of land, other than the hut-keepers and
young inexperienced stockmen that had stayed up here for a couple
of seasons to establish a claim, squatting in a hut, running a few cattle, showing the blacks they'd come and intended to stay and had
best not be interfered with.

When we come it was to settle. To manage and work a run of a
thousand acres, unfenced and not marked out save on a map that
wouldn't have covered more than a square handkerchief of it and
could show nothing of what it was. How black the soil, how coarse
and green the grass and stunted the scrub and how easy a mob can
get lost in it. Or how the heat lies over it like a throbbing cloud all
summer, and how the blacks are hidden away in it, ghosts that in
those days were still visible and could stop you in your tracks.

Mr McIvor, who owned the run, had no thought of coming up
here himself. He was too comfortable out at Double Bay, him and his
wife and two boys in boots and collars that I saw when I went out
with Pa to get our instructions. I talked to them a bit, and the older
one asked me if I could fight, but only asked; he didn't want to try it.
This was in a garden down a set of wooden steps to the water, with
a green lawn and a hammock, and lilies on green stalks as long as
gun barrels, red.

Mr McIvor meant to stay put till the land up here was secured
and settled and made safe. He might come up then and build a
homestead. Meantime, my pa was to be superintendent, with a
wage of not much more than a roof over our heads and a box of provisions that come up every six months by bullock dray, eleven days
from the coast. To hold on to the place and run the mob he had
stocked it with.

Our nearest neighbours were twelve miles off, southwest, and
had blacks to work for them out of a mob that had settled on the
creek below their hut. We only heard of this, not seen it. We had just

ourselves. Pa believed it was better that way, we relied on nobody but ourselves. It was the way he liked it. Ourselves and no other. He wouldn't have slept easy with blacks in a mob close by, in a camp
45 and settled. Maybe wandering in and out of the yards, or the hut even, and sleeping close by at night. Or not sleeping.

"You trust nobody, boy, there's nobody'll look out for you better'n yourself. I learned that the hard way. I'm learnin' it to you the easy way, if you'll listen. We're on our own out here. That's the best way
50 to be. No one watchin', or complainin' about this or that you done wrong, or askin' you to do it their ways. Just us. We're on to a good thing this time. We'll make it work. Damn me if we won't!"

There had been other places, a good many of them, where it didn't work. He had no luck, Pa. After a time there was always
55 some trouble. There was something in the work he was asked to do, or the way the feller asked it, got his goat, and irked or offended him. He'd begin to walk round with that set, ill-used look to him that you knew after a time to avoid, and I would hear him, low and sulky, complaining to Ma after they had gone to bed. You could hear
60 the aggrievement in his voice and the stubbornness and pride in his justifications.

I don't know when I first begun to see he wasn't always in the right. I might have picked it up in the first instance from Ma, from her silence, or from the way she'd start packing up her bits and
65 pieces, things she had had from way back before I was born – a tea caddy made of tin with little pigtailed Chinamen on it, a good-sized greenish stone from the Isle of Skye, which is where she was from – them and whatever else she had an affection for and had saved out of our many wrecks. She had already begun to pack them up in her
70 head before he even come out with it, that we were on the move again.

"I won't be treated like a bloody nigger," he'd be telling her. "A man's got a right to a bit of respect." I don't know how many times I heard him say that, and saw the fierce look he wore, and felt the air
75 hiss out of him and saw the scared look in her eye.

It was his pride. His impatience, too. Something in him that made doing things another man's way impossible to him.

I never once heard him put it down to anything he had done himself, to the trouble he had knuckling under or settling. It was always
80 someone else was to blame. Or some power of bad luck or malice against him that all his life had dogged and downgraded him, going right back, and which he saw in the many forms it took to bring him low. In a look on one feller's face that said: "This work is not done the way I want it. It is not to my liking. Do it again. An' if you can't

do it my way, then we'd better part company." Or in a finger mov- 90
ing slowly up a column of figures, and a frown that said: "Hello,
what's this?" Then that cloud of old hurt and misjustice on his face
for being once again doubted and disrespected, and while he raged
and justified, the bundling up, all in a rush, of our few bits of things.

Always the same end to every venture, no matter how hopeful he 95
started out: anger and disappointment. But what I saw on those occasions was more than disappointment. It was shame. In front of
Ma, and of me too I think, once he begun to consider me. At having
so little power to hold us in one place and safe. At being always at
the mercy of another man's discontents. 100

He wasn't always right. But Ma did not once, that I ever heard,
cross him or argue back. We stuck together. We were loyal. If I
learned that, it was not so much from what he told me of the neces-
sity of it, which he did often enough, but from watching her.

Whatever strung the different places together was in what she 105
made. In the first meal we ate there, the plates set out the same way
as at the last meal we'd sat down to, and a bit later the line of clothes
she'd have drying, with the wind of the new place lifting and puff-
ing them full of sunlight. In the smile she'd allow herself when he
told her, with all his old false confidence: "This is a good place, Ef – 110
an' he's a good man, I reckon. This'll do us for a bit – what d'you
say?"

But I'd noticed something else by then. That people somehow,
where he was concerned, were not well-disposed, they were not
kindly. He lacked whatever it is that makes people respond. 115

Maybe he was just too much himself. Too ungiving. Or maybe the
opposite – he wasn't ready enough to receive. Anyway, he could
never get it right, never manage to ask for a thing in a way that won
men over. He'd ask and they'd frown and hum and shift their feet in
the dirt, and he'd already have took offence or temper before they'd 120
even come up with an answer. They'd feel then that they'd been
right to hold back, and him that he had been a fool ever to ask.

He also discovered after a while, and long before I even knew
what it was, that I did have it – the power, whatever it is, to soften
people, win them over. He'd get me to ask for things he knew no 125
amount of asking on his part could get him, and laugh up his sleeve
at the way they'd been hooked. And even if it was a gift he despised
and wouldn't have wanted for himself, he was happy for me to
make use of it. He'd just stand there and listen while I soft-soaped
them, and I could tell from the way he looked and smiled to himself, 130
but it was a sour smile, that he scorned me. He was pleased I could
do it, but it was something in me that he scorned and might come to

hate in the long run – that's what I thought. He didn't know how I'd
got hold of it, where it had come from. Not from him, not from his
135 blood. So I needed all the more to stick close and show him, whatever he thought, that there was connection. That I was loyal, blood-
loyal, and always would be, come whatever. Whatever.

It was blacksoil country, and when the rains come, all mud. The
land flowed then like a river as wide as the horizon in all directions.
140 In the dry it was baked hard, and cracked. The low scrub got so
green that the light of it hurt your eyes, and when the grass sprung
up it was a lawn for two or three days, like Mr McIvor's lawn out at
Double Bay, then it was swaying round your knees and next thing
you knew the cattle were lost in it. He cursed it and had a complaint
145 about every aspect of it. Most of all about the blacks, as if all the
faults of the country were their doing. As if they'd made it the way
it was.

"They'd better keep clear a' this place, that's all I got to say," people. Our neighbours the Jolleys, for instance, the one or two times
150 we met.

"Oh, the blacks are all right if you treat 'em right," Mick Jolley
would say.

"Yair," he'd say, "well, my idea of treatin' 'em right is to keep 'em
where they bloody belong. Which is not on my property. Not while
155 I'm in charge of it." And he spat, and wiped the sweat off his face
with a red handkerchief he wore, and screwed his eyes up against
the glare of green.

Fact is, I loved this place we'd come to. Better than any other
we'd been in.

160 He didn't. Not really. Nor Ma neither. For her it was a kind of
horror, I knew that, though she would never have admitted it.

It was further out than we'd been before, and for her it was too
far. All the things that tied her to the world – a store where she
could turn things over at a counter, even if she couldn't afford to
165 buy, a bit of material or that to pass through her fingers, a bit of talk,
the sight of other women and what they were wearing – a new style
of bonnet or the cut of a pair of shoes. All that, and the comfort of
neighbours, of being linked that way, was gone. She went out only
to hang the wash on the line, and even then I don't believe she ever
170 raised her eyes to the country. She just acted as if it wasn't there.

But I loved it.

This is my sort of country, I thought, the minute I first laid eyes
on it. And the more I explored out into it the more I felt it was made
for me and just set there, waiting.

It was more than it looked. You had to give it a chance to show it-   175
self. There were things in it you had to get up close to, if you were to
see what they really were – down on your knees, then sprawled out
flat with your chest and your kneecaps touching it, feeling its grit.
Then you could see it, and smell the richness of it, too, that only
come to your nostrils otherwise after a good fall of rain, when the   180
smells were in the steam that rose up for just seconds and were
gone.

Most of all I liked the voices of it. The day voices, magpies and
crows and the rattle of cicadas, and the night voices, spotted night-
jars calling caw-caw-caw gabble-gabble-gabble, and owls, and frogs   185
I had never seen by day but heard after dark, so I knew they must be
there, and found them at last, so small it was no wonder I'd missed
them, and with the trick of taking on the colour, green or stripy-
bark-like, of whatever they were clamped to, and only their eyes
catching the light like tiny dewdrops, liquid and gleaming, till they   190
blinked.

Nothing in it scared me. Not even the tiger snakes or diamond-
heads you saw basking in the sun, then slithering off between hiss-
ing stems.

After a bit I would get up nights, let myself out and lie in some   195
place out there under the stars. Letting the sounds rise up all around
me in the heat, and letting a breeze touch me, if there was one, so I
felt the touch of it on my bare skin like hands.

Keeping the blacks off the land was a difficult proposition. Little
groups of them – women and children dawdling along and chatting   200
as they dug with sticks, bands of fellers on a hunting party – were
forever straying across what we knew were our rightful boundaries.

Pa would put up with it for a bit, then go out with a gun and
shout at them. There would be scowls and mutterings, and a shaking of spears on their side if it was the men, and on our side Pa,   205
standing square and hard-mouthed, showing no fear, whatever he
might have felt, with his shotgun across his arm.

He didn't have to point it. It was enough that he had it across his
arm. They knew by now what it could do.

They were noisy and fierce-looking, them fellers, but it was show;   210
and so on Pa's side was the shotgun. Only our show was more con-
vincing, I reckon. Our noise, if it come to that, would be a single
blast. Louder than anything they could produce, and they knew it.
Louder, and from a darker place than a mere mouth.

I think Pa liked what it felt like to just stand there and watch   215
them fellers dance and shout, singing out loud enough, but power-

less. It made him all the quieter, just standing and watching how the puff went out of them after a bit. One or two of the fiercer ones among them would make a run, but only two or three steps, and he'd stand his ground, smiling to himself, no need to react.

It was a feeble token. They'd already decided to back off. And when they did, slinking off one by one and throwing dark looks over their shoulder, and muttering, he'd keep standing. I think it was the best he ever got to feel maybe in his life, being left like that facing the empty bush, the last one in the field.

If it was a bunch of just women and little kids he didn't even bother to confront them. He'd just fire the shotgun once in the air, and laugh at the way they squealed and run about rounding up their kids, then scattered.

Most of the time I was there beside him, since most of the work to be done round the place we did together. I was his off-sider, his chief helper. We had no others.

I was too half-grown and scrawny to offer him much physical support, but me being not yet a grown man, even by their lights, was a constraint on them, and in that I gave him an advantage he didn't maybe appreciate. I know this because when I didn't have any jobs to do for Ma, and wasn't out working with him, I'd wander off alone and pass right close to them and all they'd do, whatever they were engaged in, was look. They never offered any word of threat. They'd just look. Like I was some curious creature that had come into view, that was of no use to them because I couldn't be hunted, and was just there – but in a way maybe that changed things and made them curious.

They didn't give me any acknowledgment, either one way or the other, except just with their long looks.

And no trouble, neither. But I'd feel the skin creep on my skull, and I'd walk on as if I was walking on eggshells or air, and I'd just whisper to Jamie, if he was with me, "Just keep on walkin', Jamie, and don't give 'em no notice," and felt there was a kind of magic around us, that come from their looking and protected us from harm. Though all it might be was us being so young.

And that day?

It seemed no different from any of the other occasions. We were in the home paddock grubbing out the last of a patch of low mulga scrub, him all strained and sweating with a rope around his middle, me with a crowbar under the dug-out roots. Suddenly he looked over my head and said quietly: "Get me gun, Jordie. Leave that now."

Aborigine hunters.
The Australian aboriginal population is now estimated at approximately 54,000, of whom approximately 33,000 still live a nomadic existence, hunting in the traditional ways.

I looked to where he was looking and didn't move quick enough
260   for him. He had slipped clear of the rope. He jerked his elbow at me
and I jumped and run. When I come back he was standing with an
odd little smile on his face. I don't think I'd ever seen him so good-
humoured, so playful-looking.

Before he took the gun from me he rubbed his palms on the side
265   of his pants; they were grimed with dirt and sweat from the rope.
Then, still smiling a little, he ran his fingers through his hair.

He had curls that sometimes flopped into his eyes. Now, with his
fingers, he smoothed them back and his bronze-coloured hair was
dark wet.

270   I handed him the gun and he kept watching while he loaded it.
He had never taken his eyes off them. But what I remember, even
more than what was happening, was the mood that was on him.
That was what was unusual. The rest was like any other occasion.
He shot me a lively look that said, "Watch this now, Jordie," as if
275   what was coming was to be the purest fun. I loved him at that moment. He was so easy. So happy-looking.

The blacks, all near naked, were striding along through the scrub-
by dust and in the heat-haze seemed to bounce on their heels and
rise up a little. To float.

280   There were three of them. The leading one carried something
slung across his shoulders; they weren't near enough yet for us to
see what it was. And there was a small mob at their back, not many.
A dozen, no more. About thirty yards back, in the scrub.

There was no way we could have known what it was. We'd had
285   no notice they were coming.

Pa put his hand up to stop them. They kept coming at the same slow
pace, their bodies swaying a little, or so it looked, as if they were
walking on air. "Stop there," he shouted. They were closer than they
had ever got before.

290   "That's far enough," he called. They were still coming.

I looked across to him then. He was all fired up, but not panicky.
Not angry neither, but he had a brightness to him I had never seen
before. It was like I could hear the blood beating in him, or maybe it
was mine. I think it was the moment in his life, so long as I had ever
295   known him, when he felt lightest, most sure of himself, most free.
Five minutes back he'd been straining his guts out over that stump,
every muscle of him strained – the sweat running out of him in
streams. He was still sweating now, but it was a glow.

He raised the gun and I thought: "He'll just fire over their heads
300   and scare them." He fired, and I saw the black, the leading one, take
off into the air a little and what he was carrying on his shoulders fly

up. And as he stumbled in mid-air and rolled towards us, the meat, the side of lamb, went rolling in front of him. Meantime, the other two were scurrying back, and the mob gave a cry, and the women begun wailing. It was done. It had happened.

Out of that slow-fired mood he was in. Which did not ebb away. So that even when he saw what he had done, and lowered the gun, he was still lightly smiling.

I was astonished. That he could stand there with the sound of the shot still in the air and all that yelling and be so cool. Inside the heat there had been a cold, clear place, and he had acted from there, lightly and without thought. It was like he had just hit on a new way of being inside his own skin, and from now on that was the way he would live, and I was the first, the very first, to get a glimpse of it. But he wasn't thinking of me. He just turned his back on the whole thing, and swaggering a little, walked away, leaving the blacks, who were quiet now, to creep forward and drag off the man who had been killed or wounded, while the side of meat just lay where it was, rolled in the dirt.

Later on I saw that it must have seemed like a good idea on Mick Jolley's part to send the blacks across like that. To show him, Pa, that they could be trusted. That he could just send them off like that with a gift and it would be delivered. Sort of a soft lesson to him. But how was he to know that that was what it was? All in a moment and with no warning. A mob of blacks just walking up where he had always resisted.

He was wrong, I know that. He was wrong every way. But I want to speak up for him too.

Even when Mick Jolley come across and yelled at him and tried to get him to pay the blacks what he called compensation, I was on his side; not just by standing there beside him, but in my heart.

He did not know that black was a messenger. Who had the right to pass through all territories without harm. How could he know that? And even if he had, he mightn't have cared anyway that it was a consideration in their world. It wasn't one in ours. That they should even have considerations – that there might be rules and laws hidden away in what was just makeshift savagery, hand-to-mouth getting from one day to the next and one place to another a little further on over the horizon – that would have seemed ridiculous to him. Given they had no place of settlement nor roof over their heads to keep the sun off, nor walls to keep out the wind and the black dust that made another duller blackness where they were already blacker than the most starless night. No clothes neither, to keep them decent, and had never raised even the skinniest runt of a

345 bean or turnip, nor turned a single clod to grow what went into their mouths, only scavenged what was there for anyone to crawl about and pick up. "Consideration," he would have said. "Consideration, thunder!"

Yet it was true. There were messengers. Given a part to play like 350 any sergeant or magistrate, and recognized as such even by strangers.

Though not by us.

Which made us, in some ways, the most strangers of all.

I don't believe he knew what he had done – the full extent of it. 355 And with all that light in his blood that made him so glowing and reckless, I don't think he would have cared.

I didn't know neither, but I felt it. A change. That change in him had changed me as well and all of us. He had removed us from protection. He had put us outside the rules, which all along, though he 360 didn't see it that way, had been their rules. The magic I'd felt when they just stood and looked, as if I was some creature like a unicorn maybe, had come from them. Now it was lifted.

These last months I had taken to going about the place with Jamie, I was just beginning to show him things, things I had discov-365 ered and knew about our bit of land that no one else did except maybe the blacks, and places no one else had ever been into, except them, when it was theirs. I don't reckon those hut-keepers and shepherds had ever been there. They were places you could only reach by letting yourself slide down a bank into a gully or pushing in un-370 der the low underbrush along a creek, so low you had to go on your knees, then on your belly. Jamie would have followed me anywhere, I knew that, but I was careful always to show him marks and signs along the way. Even when he was too little to talk, he was quick to see, and knew the signs again on the way back. He had known no 375 other place than this. There were times, little as he was, when I felt he was showing it to me. Only now I kept a good eye open when we were out together. The whole country had a new light over it. I had to look at it in a new way. What I saw in it now was hiding-places. Places where they were hidden in it, the blacks. Places too where 380 ghosts might be, also hidden.

The story I have been telling up till now is my story. But at this point it becomes his. Pa's.

It is the story of a twelve-year-old boy treacherously struck down in the bush by unknown hands, his body hidden away in the heart 385 of the country and for days not found, though many search-parties go looking.

The mother is distraught. She has only one woman to comfort her. All the rest of those who gather at the hut, take a hasty breakfast and set out in small groups to scour the countryside, are men, embarrassed to a profound silence by the depth of her grief. Only when they have stepped into the sunlight again, to where their horses stand restless in the sun, do they let their breath out and express what they feel in head-shaking, then anxious whispers.

They feel a kind of shyness in the presence of the father as well, but there are forms for what they can say to him. They clap him roughly on the shoulder, and impressed by the rage he is filled with, which they see as the proper form for his grief, they reach for words that will equal his in their stern commitment, their vehemence.

He is a man who has been touched by fate, endowed with the dignity of outrage and a cause. It draws together, in a tight knot, qualities that they felt till now were scattered in him and not reliable. When the body comes to light at last, the skull caved in, the chest and thighs bearing the wound-marks of spears, and he rides half-maddened about the country urging them to ride with him and kill every black they come across, he inspires in them such a mixture of horror and pity that they feel they too have been lifted out of the ordinary business of clearing scrub and rounding up cattle and are called to be heroic.

He is a figure now. That is why it is his story. The whole country is his, to rage up and down in with the appeal of his grief. His brow like thunder, his blue eyes bleared with weeping, he speaks low (he has no need to shout) of blood, of the dark pull of it, of its voice calling from the ground and from all the hidden places of the country, for the land to be cleared at last of the shadow of blood. He is a new man. He has discovered one of the ways at last to win other men to him and he blazes with the power it brings him. He is monstrous. And because he believes so completely in what he must do, is so filled with the righteous ferocity of it, others too are convinced. They are drawn to him as to a leader.

One clear cool act, the shedding of a little blood, and all that old history of slights and humiliations, of being ignored and knocked back, of having to knuckle under and be subservient – all that is cancelled out in the light he sees at last in other men's eyes, in their being so visibly in awe of the distinction that has descended upon him.

But that little blood was my blood, not just that black fella's. Pa's blood too. So he did come to see at last that I was connected.

For a season my name was on everyone's lips, most of all on his, and in the newspapers at Maitland and Moreton Bay and beyond.

430 Jordan McGivern. A name to whip up fear and justified rage and the unbridled savagery of slaughter. For a season.

The blacks in every direction are hunted and go to ground. They too have lost their protection – what little they had of it. And me all that while lying quiet in the heart of the country, slowly sinking into
435 the ancientness of it, making it mine, grain by grain blending my white grains with its many black ones. And Ma, now, at the line, with the blood beating in her throat, and his shirts, where she has just pegged them out, beginning to swell with the breeze, resting her chin on a wet sheet and raising her eyes to the land and gazing off
440 into the brimming heart of it.

Annotations

7 **dent** (n.): a hollow area in the surface of something, usually made by sth. hitting it – 9 **I been**: (sl. for) I have been – 10 **come up**: (sl. for) came up – 12 **stockman** (n.): a man whose job it is to look after farm animals – 13 **squatting**: living in a building or on a piece of land without permission and without paying rent – 19 **coarse** (adj.): (here) rough – 20 **scrub** (n.): low bushes and trees that grow in very dry soil, often implying poor quality vegetation – **mob** (n.): (in AustrE and NZE) a large group of sheep or cattle – 24 **run** (n.): the land, the farm property – 25 **DOUBLE BAY**: a wealthy Sydney suburb on the harbour – 30 **hammock** (n.): a thing for sleeping in, consisting of a long piece of cloth or a net that is hung between two trees; (here used to imply leisure and wealth) – 36 **bullock** (n.): a young male cow that cannot breed – **dray** (n.): a flat cart with four wheels that was used in the past for carrying heavy loads, esp. barrels of beer (here in this rural context more likely to be farm produce) – 37 **mob** (n.): (AustrE and NZE) (here) a group of Aborigines (expression not necessarily derogatory; but probably so in this context of the story) – 44 **easy**: (sl.) easily – 47 **nobody'll**: nobody will – **better'n**: better than – 48 **learnin'**: (sl. misuse for) teaching – 50 **watchin' ... complainin' ... askin'**: (sl. misuse for) watching ... complaining ... asking – 51 **ways**: (sl.) way – 56 **feller** (n.): (infml.) fellow – **got his goat**: popular expression for 'really annoyed him' – **irked**: annoyed, irritated – 60 **aggrievement**: (incorrect nominal word formation) from aggrieve (v.) to express the feeling or showing of anger and unhappiness because you think you have been unfairly treated; distress – 62 **begun**: (sl.) began – 65 **tea caddy** (n.): a small box for storing tea – 67 **THE ISLE OF SKYE**: a place in Scotland – 79 **knuckle under** (phrasal verb): (infml.) to accept s.o.'s authority or orders without wanting to – 80 **malice** (n.): (here) active ill-will; the desire or inten-

tion to deliberately harm s.o. – 81 **dogged**: (here) followed, pursued (cf. "like a dog follows you") – 92 **misjustice**: (not a proper word) (here) injustice – 93 **disrespected**: (not a proper word) (here) people show him lack of respect – 95 **venture** (n.): (here) a new activitiy, a new attempt to earn a living – 100 **discontent** (n.): causes of unhappiness, anger – 110 **Ef**: his wife's name – 111 **an' he's a good man**: the boss is a good man – 120 **took offence**: (s.) taken offence – 127 **despise** (v.): dislike very much – 129 **soft-soap** (v.): (infml.) to say nice things to s.o. in order to persuade them to do sth., change their mind etc. – 131 **scorn** (v.): to treat with contempt – 143 **swaying**: moving slowly from one side to another – 148 **clear a'**: (vernacular) clear of – **I**: I've – 153 **Yair**: yes – **treatin' 'em**: (colloq.) treating them – 167 **bonnet** (n.): a type of hat that women wore in the past which tied under their chin and often had a wide brim – 183 **magpie** (n.): a bird with black and white feathers and a long tail – 190 **dewdrop** (n.): a small drop of dew (dew= the small drops of water that form on outdoor surfaces during the night) – 193 **slither** (v.): to slide smoothly across a surface, twisting or moving from side to side – 199 **proposition** (n.): task, idea; suggestion; judgement, statement – 200 **dawdle**: take a long time to do sth. or go somewhere – 204 **scowl** (n.): an angry or disapproving expression on someone's face – **muttering** (n.): complaints about sth. or expressions of doubts about it, but without saying clearly and openly what you think – 218 **puff** (n.): sudden small movement of wind, air, or smoke – 221 **feeble** (adj.): extremely weak – 222 **slinking off**: moving somewhere quietly and secretly, esp. because you are afraid or ashamed; leaving in this way – 228 **squeal**: make a long loud high sound or cry – 233 **scrawny** (adj.): thin, unattractive, and looking weak – 246 **creep** (v.): to move slowly and quietly – 254 **MULGA** (n.): (AustrE) any of various Australian acacia shrubs, esp. Acacia aneura, which grows in the central desert regions and has leaflike leafstalks; here: a particular part of the Australian bush or scrub comprised of a dense growth of acacia; also general term for the Australian outback and bush – 256 **crowbar** (n.): a heavy iron bar (bar= here: length of iron metal) used to lift or open things – 264 **palm** (n.): the inside surface of your hand between the base of your fingers and your wrist – 277 **striding**: walking quickly with long steps – 278 **bounce** (v.): to move up and down – 296 **straining his guts out**: trying as hard as possible to do sth. – 304 **scurrying**: moving quickly with short steps – 306 **Out … away**: (here) "poetic prose"; strictly speaking an incomplete sentence meaning "it had emerged out of " – 332 **that black was a messenger**: that Aborigine was a messenger; as a messenger, in Aboriginal custom, he had the right to pass freely through another's territory –

337 **makeshift savagery**: this expression implies, incorrectly, that the Aborigines here "savages" do not have a settled or systematic life style or culture – **makeshift** (adj.): made for temporary use when you need something and there is nothing better available – **savagery** (n.): extremely cruel and violent behaviour – **hand-to-mouth**: (here) not storing for the future (same connotation as makeshift savagery) – 344 **runt** (n.): (here) the smallest and least developed plant of a group of beans or turnips – **the skinniest runt of a bean or turnip**: (here) not even the smallest one – 345 **clod** (n.): lump of mud or earth – 346 **scavenge** (v.): to search through things that other people do not want for food or useful objects – 361 **unicorn** (n.): an imaginary animal like a white horse with a long straight horn growing on its head – 369 **gully** (n.): a small valley made by a creek or river – 370 **underbrush**: low branches of trees and shrubs – 383 **treacherously**: unfairly betraying trust – 387 **distraught** (adj.): so upset and worried that you cannot think clearly – 389 **scour** (v.): to search very carefully and thoroughly through an area, a document, etc – 426 **fella**: fellow, man – 429 **MAITLAND AND MORETON BAY**: places in New South Wales and Queensland

Questions

1   The opening paragraph describes the country in a very unusual way, for example as "crowded with ghosts." How does this kind of description make you feel? How would you describe the boy's relationship to the country? Look for other parts of the story where the boy's feelings for the country are described in a similar manner.

2   Try to find another historical event where people of two different cultures, races or religions have come into contact. Try writing an account of the contact from the perspective of the two different parties.

3   The third section of the story describes the relationship between the family and the local blacks (Aborigines). The narrator says that the Aborigines "were forever straying across what we knew were *our rightful boundaries.*" Make notes relating this expression to the main themes of the story.

4   How do you respond to the last section of the story? What is the effect of having the boy telling the story, even after his apparent death?

5   Consider the final paragraph. The boy talks of blending with the country, "making it mine" – try to explain what you think this suggests about "belonging" to the new land. How do you feel about the very last image, of the mother – what meanings or emotions are suggested here?

5 | Gerald Murnane

Gerald Murnane was born in Melbourne in 1939 and has lived all his life there. He studied briefly to become a Catholic priest but left to train as a primary school teacher. He then studied for a University degree and later became a college lecturer. His first novel was *Tamarisk Row* (1974), followed by *A Lifetime on Clouds* (1976). His reputation was established with a series of novels and short stories published in the 1980s and 1990s: *The Plains* (1982), *Landscape with Landscape* (1987), *Inland* (1988), *Velvet Waters* (1990) and *Emerald Blue* (1995). He received the Patrick White Award for his literary achievements in 1999.

Murnane tends to be a very private writer and does not appear very often at literary events or other similar occasions. His novels and stories might seem rather private, too. They often present us with mysteries or intellectual puzzles; they frequently make us uncertain about what is reality and what is dream or fantasy. He does not present us with an everyday world described in a realistic fashion. Instead, Murnane explores the role of the imagination and language. He has been linked to the style of writing called "magic realism" represented by writers such as Gabriel Garçia Marquez, or a writer like Jose Luis Borges, where a strange or magical world is created but the writer tells the story as if this strange world was just as normal and real as our own.

Murnane's stories suggest that our language doesn't just *describe* the world we see. He suggests instead that our language *creates* the world that we see and that our sense of reality will be influenced by our language, our culture, our experience. The world of reality is not just "out there" it is also inside, in our minds and the words we use.

Murnane uses this approach very effectively in "Land Deal" to explore an actual historical event and to the change the way we might think about it. The historical event which is the starting point of the story concerns John Batman (1801-1839), one of the first white settlers in the region where Melbourne is today. Batman entered into a treaty with the local Aboriginal chiefs. As the quotation at the start of the story shows, he exchanged blankets, knives, beads etc. for large areas of land. At least, that was how he understood the "deal." Batman is supposed to have said that "this will be the place for a village" (Murnane's story refers to this word), and he used to be seen as one of the founders of Melbourne.

In Australian history we have had the story from Batman's perspective. Murnane tells the story from the Aboriginal perspective. He doesn't attempt to recreate an accurate sense of how Aborigines in the 1830s might have reacted to the transaction. Rather he tries to imagine the logic of the deal from an Aboriginal perspective. In doing so, he challenges our ability to follow his imagination into a new and unfamiliar way of thinking; however one which seems to be quite logical in its own terms.

The story-teller says that the new European goods (the blankets, knives etc.) were *not* unfamiliar to them, because although they had never seen them before in a physical sense, they had dreamed of them. Suddenly things that had once belonged only to the "possible," things they had only dreamed of, had become "actual," real things. He decides that this can't be true, because it has never happened before. Therefore they must all be dreaming. The white men, it thus seems, did not really exist; the Aborigines only dreamt them (that explains why they were so white, because they were dreamt in a hurry!).

The logic takes many more twists and turns before we get to the end of the story. The Aborigines decide that the explanation is not that they are dreaming, but that someone is dreaming of them. Thus, they are characters in s.o. else's dreams. Such a strange explanation seems the only logical way of explaining the strange events of the meeting with the white men. The Aborigines know that it must be a dream because of one important fact, that is the white people seem to think that they can *possess* the land. From the Aboriginal perspective, this is the most absurd idea. Everyone knows that land cannot be possessed!

Murnane thus forces us, at the end of the story, into thinking about the conflict between the European and Aboriginal way of understanding ownership or possession of land. By putting us into the mind of a foreign way of thinking, he makes us think about how our own values and ideas must also look strange and even ridiculous to people from different cultures. He even suggests that the Europeans one day will have to wake up from their "dream" of owning this land.

LAND DEAL

After a full explanation of what my object was, I purchased two large tracts of land from them – about 600,000 acres, more or less – and delivered over to them blankets, knives, looking-glasses, tomahawks, beads, scissors, flour, etc., as payment for the land, and also agreed to give them a tribute, or rent, yearly.   5

John Batman, 1835

We certainly had no cause for complaint at the time. The men from overseas politely explained all the details of the contract before we signed it. Of course there were minor matters that we should have queried. But even our most experienced negotiators were distracted by the sight of the payment offered us.   10

The strangers no doubt supposed that their goods were quite unfamiliar to us. They watched tolerantly while we dipped our hands into the bags of flour, draped ourselves in blankets, and tested the blades of knives against the nearest branches. And when they left we were still toying with our new possessions. But what we mar-   15
velled at most was not their novelty. We had recognised an almost miraculous correspondence between the strangers' steel and glass and wool and flour and those metals and mirrors and cloths and foodstuffs that we so often postulated, speculated about, or dreamed of.   20

Is it surprising that a people who could use against stubborn wood and pliant grass and bloody flesh nothing more serviceable than stone – is it surprising that such a people have become so familiar with the idea of metal? Each one of us, in his dreams, had felled tall trees with blades that lodged deep in the pale pulp be-   25
neath the bark. Any of us could have enacted the sweeping of honed metal through a stand of seeded grass or described the precise parting of fat or muscle beneath a tapered knife. We knew the strength and sheen of steel and the trueness of its edge from having so often called it into possible existence.   30

It was the same with glass and wool and flour. How could we not have inferred the perfection of mirrors – we who peered so often into rippled puddles after wavering images of ourselves? There was no quality of wool that we had not conjectured as we huddled under stiff pelts of possum on rainy winter evenings. And every day   35
the laborious pounding of the women at their dusty mills recalled for us the richness of the wheaten flour that we had never tasted.

But we had always clearly distinguished between the possible and the actual. Almost anything was possible. Any god might reside behind the thundercloud or the waterfall, any faery race inhabit the land below the ocean's edge; any new day might bring us such a miracle as an axe of steel or a blanket of wool. The almost boundless scope of the possible was limited only by the occurrence of the actual. And it went without saying that what existed in the one sense could never exist in the other. Almost anything was possible except, of course, the actual.

It might be asked whether our individual or collective histories furnished any example of a possibility becoming actual. Had no man ever dreamed of possessing a certain weapon or woman and, a day or a year later, laid hold of his desire? This can be simply answered by the assurance that no one among us was ever heard to claim that anything in his possession resembled, even remotely, some possible thing he had once hoped to possess.

That same evening, with the blankets warm against our backs and the blades still gleaming beside us, we were forced to confront an unpalatable proposition. The goods that had appeared among us belonged only in a possible world. We were therefore dreaming. The dream may have been the most vivid and enduring that any of us had known. But however long it lasted it was still a dream.

We admired the subtlety of the dream. The dreamer (or dreamers – we had already admitted the likelihood of our collective responsibility) had invented a race of men among whom possible objects passed as actual. And these men had been moved to offer us the ownership of their prizes in return for something that was itself not real.

We found further evidence to support this account of things. The pallor of the men we had met that day, the lack of purposes in much of their behaviour, the vagueness of their explanations – these may well have been the flaws of men dreamed of in haste. And, perhaps paradoxically, the nearly perfect properties of the stuffs offered to us seemed the work of a dreamer, someone who lavished on the central items of his dream all those desirable qualities that are never found in actual objects.

It was this point that led us to alter part of our explanation for the events of that day. We were still agreed that what had happened was part of some dream. And yet it was characteristic of most dreams that the substance of them seemed, at the time, actual to the dreamer. How, if we were dreaming of the strangers and their goods, were we able to argue against our taking them for actual men and objects?

We decided that none of us was the dreamer. Who, then, was? One of our gods, perhaps? But no god could have had such an acquaintance with the actual that he succeeded in creating an illusion of it that had almost deceived us.

There was only one reasonable explanation. The pale strangers, the men we had first seen that day, were dreaming of us and our confusion. Or, rather, the true strangers were dreaming of a meeting between ourselves and their dreamed-of-selves.

At once, several puzzles seemed resolved. The strangers had not observed us as men observe one another. There were moments when they might have been looking through our hazy outlines towards sights they recognised more easily. They spoke to us with, oddly raised voices and claimed our attention with exaggerated gestures as though we were separated from them by a considerable distance, or as though they feared we might fade altogether from their sight before we had served the purpose for which they had allowed us into their dream.

When had this dream begun? Only, we hoped, on that same day when we first met the strangers. But we could not deny that our entire lives and the sum of our history might have been dreamed by these people of whom we knew almost nothing. This did not dismay us utterly. As characters in a dream, we might have been much less at liberty than we had always supposed. But the authors of the dream encompassing us had apparently granted us at least the freedom to recognise, after all these years, the simple truth behind what we had taken for a complex world.

Why had things happened thus? We could only assume that these other men dreamed for the same purpose that we (dreamers within a dream) often gave ourselves up to dreaming. They wanted for a time to mistake the possible for the actual. At that moment, as we deliberated under familiar stars (already subtly different now that we knew their true origin), the dreaming men were in an actual land far away, arranging our very deliberations so that their dreamed-of-selves could enjoy for a little while the illusion that they had acquired something actual.

And what was this unreal object of their dreams? The document we had signed explained everything. If we had not been distracted by their glass and steel that afternoon we would have recognised even then the absurdity of the day's events. The strangers wanted to possess the land.

Of course it was the wildest folly to suppose that the land, which was by definition indivisible, could be measured or parcelled out by a mere agreement among men. In any case, we had been fairly sure

that the foreigners failed to see our land. From their awkwardness
125 and unease as they stood on the soil, we judged that they did not recognise the support it provided or the respect it demanded. When
they moved even a short distance across it, stepping aside from
places that invited passage and treading on places that were plainly
not to be intruded on, we knew that they would lose themselves be-
130 fore they found the real land.

Still, they had seen a land of some sort. That land was, in their own
words, a place for farms and even, perhaps, a village. It would have
been more in keeping with the scope of the dream surrounding them
had they talked of founding an unheard-of city where they stood. But
135 all their schemes were alike from our point of view. Villages or cities
were all in the realm of possibility and could never have a real existence. The land would remain the land, designed for us yet, at the
same time, providing the scenery for the dreams of a people who
would never see either our land or any land they dreamed of.

140 What could we do, knowing what we then knew? We seemed as
helpless as those characters we remembered from private dreams
who tried to run with legs strangely nerveless. Yet if we had no
choice but to complete the events of the dream, we could still admire the marvellous inventiveness of it. And we could wonder end-
145 lessly what sort of people they were in their far country, dreaming of
a possible land they could never inhabit, dreaming further of a people such as ourselves with our one weakness, and then dreaming of
acquiring from us the land which could never exist.

We decided, of course, to abide by the transaction that had been
150 so neatly contrived. And although we knew we could never truly
awake from a dream that did not belong to us, still we trusted that
one day we might seem, to ourselves at least, to awake.

Some of us, remembering how after dreams of loss they had awa-
kened with real tears in their eyes, hoped that we would somehow
155 wake to be convinced of the genuineness of the steel in our hands
and the wool round our shoulders. Others insisted that for as long
as we handled such things we could be no more than characters in
the vast dream that had settled over us – the dream that would
never end until a race of men in a land unknown to us learned how
160 much of their history was a dream that must one day end.

Annotations

3 **tomahawks** (n., pl.): a small hand held axe – **bead** (n.): one of a set
of small, usually round pieces of glass, wood, plastic etc, that you
can put on a string and wear as jewellery – 9 **query**: to question –

13 **drape** (v.): to cover s.o. or sth. with folds of cloth – 14 **blade** (n.): the flat cutting part of a tool or weapon – 19 **foodstuff** (n.): a word meaning food, used esp. when talking about the business of producing or selling food – 22 **pliant** (adj.): easy to bend without breaking or cracking – **serviceable** (adj.): useful – 25 **pulp** (n.): (here) the soft inside part of a tree; wood or other substances from plants that are used for making paper – 26 **honed**: sharpened – 28 **tapered** (adj.): having a shape that gets narrower towards one end – 29 **sheen** (n.): a soft smooth shiny appearance – **trueness** (n.): (here) sharpness – 33 **ripple**: small wave, (here) a puddle displaying small movements (= resembling little waves) on the surface – **puddle** (n.): a small pool of water, esp. rainwater, on a path, road etc. – 34 **conjecture** (v.): imagine; guess – 35 **pelt** (n.): the skin or fur of a dead animal – **possum** (n.): one of various types of small furry animals that climb trees and live in America or Australia – 36 **pounding** (n.): the action of sth. repeatedly hitting a surface very hard – 40 **faery** (n.): (or faerie: old-use for) a fairy (= a small imaginary creature with magic powers, which looks like a very small person) – 43 **scope** (n.): size, extent – 44 **to go without saying**: being obvious and apparent, sth. can be taken for granted – 51 **assurance** (n.): promise, guarantee – 56 **unpalatable** (adj.): very unpleasant and difficult to accept – 60 **subtlety** (n.): (here) richness, complexity – 67 **pallor** (n.): unhealthy paleness of the skin or face – 70 **stuffs** (n., pl.): (infml.) materials, products – 71 **lavish** (v.): (here) to give or spend generously – 101 **dismay** (v.): disappoint, upset – 104 **encompassing**: including – 111 **deliberate** (v.): to think about sth. very carefully – 121 **folly** (n.): a very stupid thing to do, esp. one that is likely to have serious results – 128 **treading on**: stepping on – 132 **A VILLAGE**: (here) refers to the historical statement of Batman, the founder of the city of Melbourne, who was supposed to have said: "This will be the place for a village" – 149 **to abide by**(-phrasal v.): to accept and obey a decision, rule, agreement etc, even though you may not agree with it – 155 **genuineness** (n.): (here) realness or authenticity

Questions

1   Murnane uses very careful, rational language as he takes us through the story step by step. Can you suggest some ideas about why he chose to write the story in this style?

2   Do you think that the story is effective in changing the way that the reader might normally think about a "historical event" of the kind it describes? If so, try to list some points saying how you think it manages to do this.

3   Try to find another historical event where people of two different cultures, races or religions have come into contact. Write an account of the contact from the perspective of the two different parties.

4   Describe in your own words the Aborigine's attitude to the land as suggested by the story.

5   What is the point Murnane is making in the story's final sentence: that the dream would never end "until a race of men in a land unknown to us learned how much of their history was a dream that must one day end"?

"A part of some dream …?" (l.76)
An old Aborigine meets with western civilisation.

6 | Lily Brett

Lily Brett was born in 1946 in a "displaced person's" camp in Germany. Her Jewish parents were survivors of the Lodz Ghetto and of the Auschwitz concentration camp. Her family moved to Melbourne in 1948, as did many refugee families following the Second World War. In 1961 she began writing for a rock music newspaper, then her many books of poetry, short stories and essays began appearing in 1986. Since 1991, Brett has lived in New York with her husband, the Australian artist David Rankin.

Many of Brett's poems deal in frank and painful ways with the experience of being the child of Holocaust survivors and living so far removed from Europe. Her short stories concentrate on the same experiences. Many have a clearly autobiographical aspect as well; however, here the treatment often involves comedy. Nevertheless, even the comedy is tinged with pathos and the memory of tragedy.

After the Second World War, the Australian government began a large-scale immigration programme. It encouraged large numbers of migrants in order to boost the Australian population for reasons of defence security and economic productivity. It accepted many refugees or displaced persons from the areas of Europe most affected by the war. Later the immigration program was extended to countries such as Italy, Greece, Turkey, and Lebanon; then, in the 1970s and 1980s, to Asian countries such as Vietnam and China. Australia now has one of the largest migrant populations of any country in the world (about 40% of Australians are migrants or the children of migrants); migrants have also come from many different countries, making Australia a "multicultural" nation. One effect of this process has been that writing by migrants and those from non-English language families, like Lily Brett, has now become an important part of Australian literature.

Brett's family belonged to one of the earliest waves of this migration. "The Holiday" is the opening story in her first book of short stories *Things Could be Worse* (1990). It describes the way in which a group of Jewish migrants from Europe meet and form a close group, "our company," in 1950, quite soon after their arrival in Australia. For one family, at least, the Bensky's, it is their first holiday in Australia. They all meet at Hepburn Springs, a holiday site with natural spring waters, in Victoria (all places mentioned in this story are real places). Later, as they become wealthier in Australia, they can afford to travel to Surfers Paradise on Queensland's Gold Coast, to New Zealand, and to Israel. Nevertheless, for all their good humour and holiday friendliness, the families are haunted by their memories.

Many of their attempts to create a new community and new families fail and in the end they are still alone and vulnerable. Australia hadn't solved their problems, and it had also taken their children away from them.

THE HOLIDAY

It was the holiday in Olinda, they all agreed, that marked the beginning of the end. Mr and Mrs Bensky, Mr and Mrs Small, Mr and Mrs Pekelman, Mr and Mrs Ganz and Mr Berman had been a group for thirty-two years. "Our company," they called themselves. Every
5 Easter and every Christmas they went somewhere together .

At first the holidays were modest. They were all migrants, newly arrived refugees, when they met in Australia. They met in the summer of 1950, at Solly Nadel's Guest House in Hepburn Springs. Mr and Mrs Bensky had arrived at Nadel's on a truck. Mrs Bensky and
10 Lola had travelled in the cabin with the driver, and Mr Bensky was strapped to a chair on the back of the truck.

Josl Bensky had paid Jack, the driver, to drive them to Hepburn Springs. In two weeks, Jack would come and pick them up and take them home. The return trip cost Josl five shillings. Mrs Bensky had
15 wept all the way there. She was sure her Josl was going to fall off the truck. And Lola, unnerved by Mrs Bensky's cries, had screamed all the way to Hepburn Springs.

When they arrived, Mr Bensky had had to wait for Jack to unstrap him. He felt a bit humiliated when a group of guests gathered
20 to watch.

It was the Benskys' first holiday in Australia. Mrs Bensky entered Lola in the fancy-dress competition. From some cardboard and newspaper and glue, and a bottle of black ink, Mrs Bensky made Lola a witch's outfit. A black pointed hat, a black fringed cloak and
25 a big false nose. Little Lola, the witch, won second prize.

By the end of the fortnight the "company" had been formed. Mr and Mrs Bensky, Mr and Mrs Small, Mr and Mrs Pekelman, Mr and Mrs Ganz and Mr and Mrs Berman had gone for walks together after dinner at night. They had bottled the mineral water from the
30 springs together. They had eaten together. They were firm friends.

Mr and Mrs Pekelman had arrived in Melbourne only four weeks earlier. Mrs Bensky took Mrs Pekelman under her wing. She introduced her to Mrs Papov and to Mrs Berg. It was essential, Renia Bensky explained to Genia Pekelman, to be on the good side of these
35 gossip-mongers.

74

Later, in Melbourne, Renia took Genia shopping. The two women bought a length of black knitted fabric from the Victoria Market. From this material, Renia made two tops with scooped necklines and three-quarter sleeves, and two straight skirts.

Renia made a whole wardrobe for herself and Mrs Pekelman. The total cost of this wardrobe was less than the price of one dress at Myers. Mrs Bensky felt very proud of herself. Mrs Pekelman was grateful, and she remained in eternal admiration of Mrs Bensky.

The two women looked so stylish, so elegant, so beautiful in their new clothes. Mrs Bensky's hair was cut in the new chic, short, gamin style. She had taught Mrs Pekelman how to roll her thick auburn hair into a chignon. Both women were olive-skinned and strong-limbed. Looking at them, it was impossible to believe that five years ago Renia Bensky was in Auschwitz and Genia Pekelman was in Bergen-Belsen.

At Solly Nadel's Guest House, the men (and an occasional woman) sat inside and played cards. One hundred and two degrees Fahrenheit, and they sat with the windows closed, the air thick with cigarette smoke. And they played cards. They played Red Aces, poker and gin rummy.

The women sat in small groups outside. They chatted to each other and fussed around their own children and other people's children. Shouldn't little Johnny be wearing a sun hat? How could Harry's mother let him out without some sunburn cream on his nose? And look at that Layla, didn't Mrs Hersh know that a young girl shouldn't be allowed to get so fat? And, the Horowitz boy, he was already out of control. What would it be like when he was a teenager? For the women on holiday, here at Solly Nadel's in Hepburn Springs, these were the questions of the day.

At night there was dancing. The guests at Solly Nadel's could be divided into six categories. The good dancers, the bad dancers and the non-dancers, and the good card-players, the bad card-players and the non-card-players.

The good dancers enjoyed the highest status at Solly Nadel's. Their importance could only be surpassed by a professor or a doctor. There were not too many professors or doctors at Solly Nadel's, so the good dancers were the élite.

"Look at that Mr Gruner, what a dancer," Genia Pekelman said almost every morning at the breakfast table. "He dances the tango and the foxtrot like he was in a world championship of dancing." Genia Pekelman, who was awkward in the kitchen and around the dinner table, turned into a light-footed, delicate slip of a girl on the dance floor. All her self-consciousness left her. She side-stepped and

75

back-stepped. She whirled in neat, graceful circles. She swivelled
80 her hips and held her head at a coquettish angle.

During the day, the ballroom at Solly Nadel's was used as a din-
ing room. Breakfast, lunch and dinner were served there. At meal
times the noise was deafening. One hundred and twenty people ate
and talked simultaneously. They ate while they talked. They talked
85 over the top of one another. If they felt they weren't being heard,
they shouted. Some of the guests shouted everything they said. The
same conversations were repeated every day. The sentiments that
were voiced were interchangeable among the guests. Mrs Bloom
would probably be saying the same thing as Mrs Fink, and Mrs
90 Freedman's thoughts often echoed Mrs Rose's.

Slivers of sentences shot through the room like crossfire. "How
old is little Esther? Oh, she's not talking yet? My Johnny says many
words. And Esther is still in nappies? What a shame. Johnny says
for quite a few weeks already, 'I need pishy. I need cucky.'"

95 Most of the men were looking for ways to better themselves. The
same conversations travelled from table to table. "Did you hear that
Mr Brown was looking for a good tailor? You can get a job at the Re-
nee of Rome Factory. He doesn't pay so good, but he always gives
the Jews work. Watch out for Mr Sal. Never do piecework for him.
100 He complains about every garment."

Every summer Solly Nadel employed Mr Muller, an elderly Aus-
trian baker, to bake bread. Mr Muller worked seven days a week in
December and January. He baked from 5 a.m. to 5 p.m. He baked
rye bread, pumpernickel and vienna, and he baked special challah
105 rolls for dinner.

There was never any bread left on the tables after the meals. Mr
Grossman saved the leftover bread from his table. After two weeks,
he took home three cardboard boxes of bread. Other people did the
same.

110 "He is a peasant, that Mr Grossman," said Mrs Lipshutz. Frieda
Factor interrupted her. "We should understand, Mrs Lipshutz, that
this is not his normal behaviour. I don't know if you know this, Mrs
Lipshutz, but Mr Grossman was in Mathausen concentration
camp." "Well, he is now in Melbourne, Australia, where there is
115 plenty of bread," Mrs Lipshutz replied. "That sort of behaviour
causes anti-Semitism," she added.

Mrs Lipshutz, who had been in Australia for ten years, was not
happy with the postwar influx of Jews. "They are a different brand
of Jew altogether," she told her Australian neighbour, Mrs Cunning-
120 ham. "They are peasants. We, Adam and I, came from cultured

families. We read books, we went to the theatre, we went to the opera, we always had the best seats. We travelled in Europe. My father spoke fluent French. We were not peasants. You will see, these Jewish refugees will make the Australian people into anti-Semites."

"Oh, no, Mrs Lipshutz," said Mrs Cunningham. "I feel so sorry for some of them. They're still young girls. With those numbers on their arms they remind me of branded cattle. And Mrs Lipshutz, I met a young woman who was a dentist in Warsaw before the war, and now she is a cleaner. And her sister, who was a doctor, is working as a machinist."

"Pheh!" said Mrs Lipshutz. "They all say that they were doctors in Poland."

Later that night, Mrs Lipshutz told Mr Lipshutz that her greatest fears had been confirmed. Mrs Cunningham, their hard-working, church-going neighbour, had told her that these new Jewish migrants looked like cattle.

"If it was so easy for a good, kind person like Mrs Cunningham to be an anti-Semite", said Morry Lipshutz, "what hope was there for the world?"

The company went to Solly Nadel's for their Christmas holidays every year until 1959. By then they had a bit more money. Things were looking up for most of the group. The Smalls and the Pekelmans were partners in a knitting factory. Mr Bensky owned Joren Fashions, a small factory that manufactured ladies' suits. Costumes, Josl called them. Pola and Moshe Ganz already had six machinists working for them at Champs Elysees Blouses, and Mr Berman wholesaled plastic bags. Joseph Zelman was the wealthiest of the group. He was already building his sixth block of flats. He bought the land, built the flats, and sold them as they were being built. He worked day and night. He undercut his competition by settling for a smaller profit. In 1959 he was on his way to banking his first million.

In 1959 the company went to Surfers Paradise. They rented four units in the same block in Cavill Avenue. Mrs Bensky brought her own frozen chicken stock. Mrs Zelman brought six pounds of lean beef, which she made into three big klops on the first day. One klops for lunch, and two for later in the week. Mrs Ganz stewed a big pot of apples and baked a sponge cake, and everyone felt at home.

They ate their meals outside, around the swimming pool. At night they walked along the beach. For Mr Bensky, the highlight of this holiday was the matzoh brei that Mrs Zelman made for everyone most mornings. Josl was the first at the breakfast table each morning. He looked so happy eating the matzoh brei that Mrs Zelman thought she could have happily made it for him forever. Some men, she thought, are so easy to please.

165 Surfers Paradise, the company decided, was a very successful holiday place. They went there often after that.

The company had other memorable holidays. They went to Rotorua in New Zealand. They had mud baths and mineral spas. Mrs Bensky loved this. She sat happily for hours covered in hot mud.
170 Josl had to be ordered into the mud. He hated it. On the second day Josl sprained his ankle, and had to spend the rest of his New Zealand holiday doing what he liked best. He lay on the bed in the motel room and read detective novels. He finished a book and a box of chocolates a day.

175 Mrs Ganz and Mr Zelman went to the mineral baths together. Mrs Bensky was worried. She feared that the attachment between them was more than it should be. No one else appeared worried.

In New Zealand the company discovered duty-free shopping. All the families came home with new cameras.

180 In 1982 the company went to Israel. They had planned this trip for months. Mr Bensky was in charge of the itinerary. They stopped in Las Vegas on their way to Israel.

Mr Bensky was one of the keenest card-players of the group. He loved to gamble. Mr Zelman and Mr Pekelman thought that Las Ve-
185 gas wasn't really on the way from Melbourne to Tel Aviv, but they kept their thoughts to themselves.

Josl Bensky was deliriously happy in Las Vegas. He lost at blackjack, he lost at roulette. He lost playing chemin de fer and five card stud poker. He played the poker machines in the main gambling
190 hall, and he played the mini poker machines in the toilets. In two days Josl Bensky lost $700. "Las Vegas," he told everyone in Melbourne when he got back, "was the best part of the trip."

"There's too many Jews here for me," said Izak Pekelman in Israel. "I don't feel so good among so many Jews." The rest of the group
195 thought that what Izak said may have sounded a little strange but, in different ways, they all knew what he meant.

Renia Bensky stayed in the hotel room with the flu for most of their three weeks in Israel. Genia Pekelman wouldn't go to the pictures, or to the theatre, or to any concerts. "If it's all the same to
200 you," she said, "I would prefer to stay in the hotel. It makes me too nervous to be with a crowd." To her husband Genia said what the others had understood she was trying to say: "Izak, I can't stand being in the middle of so many Jews. It makes me too nervous. What

if someone starts to shoot at us? It reminds me too much of too many things." 205

George Small couldn't eat anything in Israel. 'This is not what we ate at home in Poland,' he said. 'This is the food of Arabs, not the food of Jews.'

In Mea Shearim, the Orthodox area of Jerusalem, Josl Bensky bellowed: "Who do they think they are, these Orthodox? What are they 210 doing? Why do they have to draw such attention to themselves? Where in the Talmud does it say you have to wear such a long black coat, and the short black trousers, and the black hats? This is the modern world, not the old world. Stupid bastards. They cause trouble for everyone. Haven't the Jews had enough trouble?" By now 215 Josl was almost in tears.

That night the company were having dinner in Jerusalem. A group of Orthodox young men came and sat at the next table. Josl looked at them and said loudly, "Oy, I'm going to vomit."

Mr Berman liked Israel. But Chaim Berman was a quiet man. He 220 always agreed with the majority. He kept to himself the elation that he felt at being in the homeland of the Jewish people. He loved the robustness of the people, the honesty, the lack of artifice. He loved the commitment and the loyalty. Chaim thought that it was a privilege to live for an ideal, and in Israel people were living for an ideal. 225 They had, Chaim Berman thought, something more valuable than central heating and new television sets.

Pola Ganz had hoped that she would be able to find Chaim Berman a new wife in Israel, but after a few days Pola decided that a Jewish woman from Melbourne might be more suitable. 230

"You have to be careful with these Israelis," she said to Ada Small. "We wouldn't want to find Chaim a wife who married him because he owns a nice house and a good business in Australia."

Ada Small agreed that they had to be careful.

The group visited a kibbutz in the Negev. They all loved the kib- 235 butz. They were very impressed by the size of the kitchen, and the laundry facilities. "Did you ever see such a stove in your life?" said Joseph Zelman. With all his blocks of flats, Joseph knew about kitchens.

"Australia is paradise," Josl Bensky said on their last night in Is- 240 rael. He raised his glass and proposed a toast to Australia. "To Australia," they all chorused.

In Israel, Renia Bensky had become increasingly agitated about Pola Ganz and Joseph Zelman. Several times, she thought, she had caught them looking at each other tenderly. 245

European immigrants to Australia on board ship in 1948

By the time she was back in Australia, Renia Bensky was sure there was a heat between Pola Ganz and Joseph Zelman. And Renia Bensky felt hot watching them.

"Poor Mina Zelman," Renia said to Josl. "She hasn't suffered enough? It wasn't enough what she did go through in Bergen-Belsen? Now she has to have a Romeo for a husband? And what about poor Moishe Ganz? Maybe he is not so intelligent as our dear Joseph Zelman, but he has always been a first-class husband to Pola. The trouble with Pola is that she doesn't know when she's got something good. She is always looking for something new. She says to me, 'Oh Reni, I've found a new hairdresser. Oh Renia, I've found a new dressmaker. Oh Renia, this manicurist is better and cheaper.' Now, whatever Joseph Zelman has got in his trousers is something Pola Ganz thinks is better than what she's got at home."

Renia knew that after the war there were strange and hasty alliances formed. Women married for security. Men married mothers. Strangers married strangers. People were starved of comfort, companionship and affection. Odd matches were made. There was not always time to wait for love.

Young girls married older men. Students married their teachers. Neighbours and cousins got married. Everyone was in a hurry to begin a normal life.

Dead wives, dead husbands and dead children were present at many of these marriage ceremonies.

Renia decided that something had to be done about Pola and Joseph. She hired a private detective. Two weeks later, the private detective gave Renia a photograph of Joseph Zelman sitting in his car outside Pola Ganz's house. Renia felt very pleased with herself.

It was Easter, and the company went to Olinda. Renia packed the photograph carefully at the bottom of her suitcase. She hadn't told Josl about the detective.

In Olinda, it seemed as though it was going to be another nice Easter break. The group settled into their holiday routine. They ate nice big breakfasts, they went for walks, they sat in the autumn sun. They had good lunches, a nap after lunch, another small walk and it was time for dinner. After dinner they played cards. After three days they were all in good spirits, and felt invigorated by the country air.

On Sunday night Renia showed Ada Small the photograph. Ada didn't say much. "Why have you got a photograph of Joseph in his car?" she asked. Renia explained the location of the photograph, and its implication.

Ada Small went straight to Pola Ganz. Pola laughed and showed the photograph to Moishe. Moishe looked carefully at the photo-
290 graph. He didn't say anything. Later, he said to Josl: "So what, what does that photograph prove? Nothing." Josl had to agree.

Nobody mentioned the photograph to Mina Zelman. "She's got enough trouble," said Ada Small. "She's so tall. At her height she would never find another husband."

295 Pola refused to speak to Renia Bensky. Renia tried to explain that she had done this for Pola's own good, but Pola wouldn't even come near her.

"If she is going to be so unintelligent about this," Renia said to Josl, "she can go to hell. I am finished with Pola Ganz."

300 The atmosphere became so unpleasant that the company left Olinda a day early.

"What was really shocking about all of this," Ada Small said to her manicurist, "was that Renia Bensky and Pola Ganz had almost been machatunim." There was no word in English for machatunim,
305 Ada explained. Machatunim was the word for the relationship be-tween a couple's parents-in-law. Renia and Pola were almost the mothers-in-law of each other's children. Renia's daughter Lina had almost married Pola's son, Sam.

There was an unspoken, unanimous decision among the com-
310 pany not to tell the children why they were no longer friends. The children had to be protected.

One of Lina's colleagues at the law firm where she worked told her that she'd heard a rumour that the rift between Renia and Pola was caused by Renia's accusations that Pola had committed adul-
315 tery with Joseph Zelman.

Sam Ganz laughed when Lina told him. "My mother, having an affair? You're joking. She goes to bed in flannel nightgowns and wears face cream, throat cream, neck cream, arm and leg cream. As a kid, I used to watch her hop into bed and wonder why she didn't
320 slip straight out again. There must be another reason Renia and Pola aren't speaking."

Mrs Zelman also wondered why Renia and Pola weren't speak-ing. Maybe Ms Ganz had done something she shouldn't have been doing with Mrs Bensky's Josl. She wouldn't put it past that Pola
325 Ganz to meddle with someone else's husband.

Mr Zelman and Mrs Ganz also stopped speaking to each other. "He was a rotten lover." Mrs Ganz said to her sister. "He wore his socks to bed."

The company collapsed. Mr Small and Mr Pekelman and Mr Berman met Mr Zelman and Mr Ganz to try and patch things up. They agreed that it was important to forgive and to forget. To make a fresh start. But the women wouldn't budge.

Moishe Ganz believed his wife, and wouldn't hear a word against her. Josl, although he thought that Renia shouldn't have interfered, knew that she didn't do it out of malice.

People took sides. Mr and Mrs Small sided with the Ganzes, and Mr and Mrs Pekelman stayed loyal to the Benskys. Chaim Berman remained friendly with everyone.

For thirty-two years the company hadn't missed a Saturday night at the pictures. Now they stopped going to the pictures. They stopped playing cards. They stopped going out for supper. They stayed at home.

Mr and Mrs Small and Mr Berman took short walks around Caulfield, but their hearts weren't in it. The Zelmans tried to learn bridge, but everyone else at the Herzl Club could play well, and they gave up. Izak Pekelman took up golf. He dropped it a week later.

At weddings, barmitzvahs, engagements and anniversaries and birthdays, people knew to put the Benskys and the Ganzes at different tables.

Genia Pekelman talked separately to Renia and Pola. She begged them to make up. She said to each of them, "Couldn't you just put this behind you and make a new start?" That approach hadn't worked with Genia's daughter Rachel, and it didn't work with Renia and Pola.

Genia tried again. "If you can't be friends, at least don't be enemies. Let us all go out together again, and maybe things will get slowly better. And we will be a group again. And people will stop talking about us. And if things are not as good as they look, at least it will look as though they are good." Genia's mother used to quote this old saying to her. It had a melodic lilt in Yiddish that got lost in the translation. Nothing that Genia Pekelman said moved Renia or Pola.

This was the price of success, thought Genia. This is what happens when you can afford to hire a private detective. Life used to be so straightforward in the old days in Melbourne, thought Genia.

When they first came to Australia, some of them had lived two families to one room. Even the most comfortably off of the group, the Smalls, lived in a room at the back of their factory.

On weekends all their children played together. Now, when Genia reminded Rachel that Jack Zelman was unattached, Rachel replied, "I hate Jack Zelman." Rachel and Jack had played together so nicely when they were small.

375 Genia had thought that she had created cousins for her Rachel and her Esther in Australia. A new family. She thought that the company and their children would regard each other as family. As cousins, aunties, uncles, nephews, nieces. As it turned out, none of their children were friends, except for Lina and Sam. And now the company themselves were no longer friends.

380 They had all ended up, Genia thought, in the same position that they had been in Germany after the war. No family. No close friends. At least they had their children. But the children were another story. Even the children had brought them troubles.

Soon, Genia thought, they would all start dying. And they would 385 die alone. One of Genia's most comforting thoughts had been that she would never have to die alone. Not like the hundreds and hundreds of dead in the streets in the ghetto.

So this is how things had turned out, thought Genia Pekelman. This is how things had turned out in the goldeneh medina, the new 390 world.

Annotations

11 **strapped**: fastened – 12 **Jack**: the name "Jack" suggests an "Anglo-Australian" rather than Jewish (all the other characters) – 14 **SHILLING** (n.): (here) a unit of money used in Australia in that period. Before February 1966 Australia used the British terminology and currency division of pounds, shillings and pence (though it had its own notes and coins). In 1966 it changed to a decimal system of dollars and cents. – 24 **fringed**: having a decorative edge with threads added to sth., esp. clothes, curtains etc – 35 **gossip-monger** (n.): s.o. who likes talking about other people's private lives – 38 **scooped neckline**(n.): scoop neck, a round, quite low neck on a woman's top – 45 **gamin**: having a boyish touch; term used to describe an attractive young, boyish and cute look, not an unattractive 'manly' look – 47 **chignon** (n.): (French) a smooth knot of hair that a woman wears at the back of her head – 55 **gin rummy** (n.): a type of rummy (= a simple card game for two people) – 77 **slip of a girl**: a small thin young person – 79 **swivel** (v.): to turn around quickly without leaving a central moving point – 91 **slivers of sentences**: small pieces or fragments of sentences – 104 **rye** (n.): a type of grain that is used for making bread and whisky; rye bread = dark bread – **CHALLAH**: (from *Hebrew "Hallah"*) bread, usu. in the form of a plaited loaf, traditionally eaten by Jews to celebrate the Sabbath –

157 **sponge cake** (n.): a light cake made from eggs, sugar, and flour but usu. no fat – 160 **MATSZOH BREI** (n.): also "matso brei"; a porridge made of a type of flat bread eaten esp. by Jewish people during Passover – 212 **TALMUD** (n.): the collection of writings that make up Jewish law about religious and non-religious life – 221 **elation** (n.): a feeling of extreme happiness and excitement – 223 **artifice** (n.): a clever trick, esp. one used to deceive s.o. – 235 **kibbutz** (n.): a type of farm in Israel where many people live and work together – 314 **adultery** (n.): sex between s.o. who is married and s.o. who is not their wife or husband – 343 **BARMITZVAH** (n.): also "bar mitzvah"; the religious ceremony held when a Jewish boy reaches the age of 13 and is considered an adult in his religion – 361 **melodic lilt** (n.): a pleasant pattern of rising and falling sound in s.o.'s voice or in music – **YIDDISH** (n.): a language based on German used by Jewish people, esp. those who are from eastern Europe

Questions

1   What does the reader learn about the life of Jewish immigrants in Australia in the story? What Jewish traditions are still important to them and what languages do they use? Give examples from the text and think about their religious and cultural significance.

2   How do the couples refer to Mr. Grossman's behaviour (cf. ll. 71f.)? What explanations do they provide and what do these reveal about the self-image and self-confidence of the Jewish immigrants in Australia? Do they form one unified ethnic group according to the text?

3   In what way are the Jewish characters in the story still haunted by their past? When and what do you learn about their past experiences in the story? How does this influence their present behaviour and what effect does it have on cross-generational relations? Support your view by citing examples from the text.

4   Think about the whole story and the search for home of the individual Jewish characters. How about their attitude towards Israel? Do you think they would be happier and feel more comfortable living there?

5   Discuss the end of the story. What is meant by "This is how things had turned out in the goldeneh medina, the new world" (ll. 262f.)? What is "the goldeneh medina" the speaker is referring to in the story? Also, find out about the origin as well as the general meaning of the phrase "the goldeneh medina" by consulting an encyclopaedia or a reference book on Jewish culture and religion in your library.

7 | John Morrison

John Morrison (1904 – 1998) was born in Sunderland, England, but migrated to Australia in 1923. In later life, he used the title *Australian by Choice* for one of his books, indicating his identification with his adopted land. He left school at fourteen, and after arriving in Australia worked at a number of manual jobs including on the wharves in Melbourne and as a gardener. His experience on the Melbourne waterfront led to some of his earliest stories, published in left-wing and trade union magazines in the 1940s. He was a member of a group in Melbourne called *The Realist Writers* who were committed to the literary techniques of realism, to writing about ordinary working-class Australians, and to socialist politics.

Morrison's stories, however, are seldom directly political. Instead, they focus on the lives of ordinary people at work and in families, sometimes in the bush, sometimes the city – especially in recognisable locations around Melbourne. He saw himself as following in the tradition of Henry Lawson in writing realist stories, in simple language, about ordinary people.

Morrison published a number of books of stories which often reflect his working life: *Sailors Belong Ships* (1947); *Black Cargo* (1955); *Twenty-Three* (1962); and *North Wind* (1982). He also published two novels, *The Creeping City* (1949) and *Port of Call* (1950). In 1986 he was awarded the Patrick White Award, a recognition of his long service to Australian literature.

He lived for many years in the Dandenongs, a low mountain range close to the eastern outskirts of Melbourne. The place names mentioned in the story "Bushfire" (first published in 1963) are nearly all actual places in this region which can be located on a map: Healesville, The Basin, Yarra Glen, Montrose, Warrandyte, Hurstbridge and so on. Because the hills still have extensive forests and farmland they are prone to bushfires in the dry summer season, especially when there are strong north winds (that means hot, dry winds in this part of Australia). There have been very destructive bushfires, especially those in Victoria on "Black Friday," as it came to be known, in 1939 when 71 people died, and more recently "Ash Wednesday" in 1983; also in 1994 in NSW on the outskirts of Sydney. Bushfires in Australian forests can spread very quickly because of the eucalyptus trees: due to their high oil content they burn very fiercely. At their worst, hot winds can carry burnt leaves and ash all the way into Melbourne city.

The story describes the events in the midst of such a bushfire in the Dandenongs. The narrator and his friend, Jim, have been fighting the fire and have the chance for a brief rest. In the middle of such hectic activity and tension, the moment of rest is quite "unreal" but it enables the narrator to observe the people and circumstances around him.

Rather than writing a story of high drama and adventure, then, Morrison focuses on the human side of the events. He tells of the Gregs, an unusual family, perhaps outcasts in the district, but on this occasion a feeling for their common humanity is strongest. He observes how a fire crew from the city, from Port Melbourne, have come to assist. He notices the old couple, the Nevinsons, shopkeepers from the city, now threatened by the fire. He reflects on the way Mrs Shields "seems different tonight."

The story gives a very detailed account of the fire, the equipment, the townships, the noise, heat, smells and activity. In this way, the story works successfully rather like a documentary film, moving from one scene to the next. But Morrison's main focus is on human behaviour and emotions. On the one hand, the story shows individuals helping each other. It shows the Australian idea of "mateship" – a word which is used to describe the bonds between men built up through working or living together. Jim is described as the narrator's "mate." On the other hand, the story also talks about the "loneliness" the narrator feels, and perhaps there's a certain sadness here as well, a feeling that human life is vulnerable, that at some level we are all alone.

Fighting a bushfire near Sydney in 1994

BUSHFIRE

It was one of the most unreal moments I've ever experienced. No doubt excessive weariness had much to do with it. That, and the inevitable relaxation that comes with the smell of victory. But more than anything else I think it was the sudden comparative quietness and isolation. There'd been so much noise, so much violence, so many people. So much blinding light, now the darkness was coming back again.

Now and then, further along the slope, the vague figure of a man with a knapsack pump showed up as he patrolled the edge of destruction. In the other direction a few people moved around the surviving home of the Gregs. At my side was the inert form of Jim, collapsed, already fast asleep.

Footfalls rustle in the dry ferns behind me, and out of the shadows comes a little girl carrying a basket and a billy. Do we want anything? She's like everybody else we've seen in three days, soiled with sweat and ashes.

Eat – no! We've been eating too often. There's always plenty of food around – the women see to that – but only time to gobble a few mouthfuls. We'd give anything to get really empty and hungry, to have a wash, and sit down to a proper meal. Drink? Incredibly, I don't want that either, but the little girl looks so disappointed that I take a cupful of the strong black tea she's carrying. She goes off down the line stumbling in the brittle ground-litter and full of importance. One of the Greg children. We saved their house, anyway.

It comes over me now, the most extraordinary sensation of loneliness I've ever known. It calls to mind something I once read. An English literary periodical asked its readers to say what they considered to be the most awful predicament a man could possibly find himself in. One of the answers stuck with me throughout the years: "To be utterly alone in infinite space."

It's something like that. A sense of terrifying emptiness, and a desolation that takes away even the comfort of my own body. I'm aware of the broken end of a fern-stalk sticking into my hip, and of something crawling along my neck. But neither one nor the other seems to concern me. Far up on the main road behind me the roar of vehicles goes on unceasingly: rural fire brigades, water-tankers, police, trucks crowded with men, pouring up to the raging southern front of the fire. But for me it's over, if only for a few minutes. I'm absorbed by the scene before me, and I sit like a man trying to fix forever the details of a fascinating dream.

Perhaps the northerly is falling at last. More likely it's still blowing; we wouldn't know down here deep on a southern slope. All I do know is that it has become very quiet, and after the sustained violence of three days it's a quietness that intimidates. Only a few
45 yards beyond my extended feet the tangle of parched ferns and wire grass stops as abruptly as along a road, and there is nothing. Little is left on the living trees, but here and there flames still sputter and glow in the high forks and along dead limbs. A stone's throw away the great hollow shell of a long-dead veteran roars like a furnace. It's
50 a good shell, straight and sound as a gun barrel, with a hole near the ground big enough for a man to crawl into. Every now and then the coals on the white-hot inner walls collapse and a blast of flames and sparks belches from the top. I know that the valley is full of such fireworks, but it's full of smoke too, and all that reaches me for a few
55 minutes is an occasional thump as another tree comes down.

Then, high in the darkness of the opposing ridge, a man suddenly calls out, and there's a clanging crash like an empty watertank falling. I didn't think there was anything left to burn up there, but they must still be fighting. The two sounds bring home to me as
60 nothing else does just what it is that has happened. I've been down here so often before, and this is the first time I've heard sounds from that ridge. Every noise carries now because there is nothing left to absorb it. The entire valley has been cleaned out. Not a leaf or a stick or a blade of grass left. It's just a huge ditch full of ashes, smoulder-
65 ing logs, naked spars, smoke, and the sad wreckage of homes.

And out of it there comes that extraordinary rustling. I'm aware of it quite suddenly, and find it rather soothing after the long crackle of flames and the clash and fury of struggling men. I'm not sure what to make of it, uncertain whether it's the snapping of millions of
70 sparks or the settling down of all these acres of cooling ash. Either way it fits in perfectly with scene and mood. An endless, whispering, papery sigh. A sigh of exhaustion. The dying down of a burned and blighted earth.

Tuesday night. It seems so long since noon on Sunday, when it came
75 over the air that a bushfire was burning at Chum Creek, near Healesville, thirty miles away. Since we heard that a second fire had broken out at The Basin, only nine miles from us on the other side of the Dandenongs. So long since Sunday afternoon when the first smoke haze drifted over, and my wife came in from the garden and
80 showed me the fine ash which had settled on her dress. Yarra Glen and Montrose on Monday, Warrandyte and Dogwood today. We're in an arc of fire extending nearly a hundred miles from Warrandyte

and Hurstbridge in the west, through St. Andrew's, Kinglake, and Healesville, to Launching Place in the east, and Ferntree Gully in the south. And many points within the arc. Only heavy rain can save what's left. And all that we're promised is a possible – just a possible – thunderstorm.

Two men come past, trudging heavily along the dampened edge of ashes. Both are carrying knapsack pumps, obviously empty. One of them looks as if, like my mate Jim, he's been in it from the start. He doesn't walk. He goes in a succession of staggers, leaning forward and catching his weight step by step. His shirt and trousers are ragged and black. One forearm is swathed in dirty bandages. Even so, he notices Jim, and stops to ask in a slurred voice: "How is he – all right?"

"Yes, he's all right," I assure him. "He's just had it."

"Ain't we all."

They pass on, but the spell is broken, and I shake Jim into life. "We'd better get up top, Jim. See what's doing."

He sits up, passes both hands across his face and spits. "Jeeze, me eyes is crook. What time is it?"

"Getting on for ten. It's safe down here now. There's a few standing by."

As we get to our feet and start off I observe the beater he's carrying. A folded potato-bag nailed to the end of a three-feet length of two by one hardwood. Half the bag charred away. It makes mine look like the tool of a novice.

Just before reaching the track that leads up to the road we get close to the Gregs' house. They're a tough crowd, source of endless gossip and speculation in the township. One man, two women, and eleven children, living in a higgledy-piggledy cluster of splintered weatherboards and rusted roofing-iron on an unfenced block. For years all the rubbish of a turbulent don't-give-a-damn household has gone into the surrounding bush, and the fire, which licked the very walls, has laid it all bare. A little way down the hillside a piped fallen tree burns safely but fiercely, lighting up the blackened litter of jam tins, shattered bottles, drums, iron bedstead, and metal remains of a derelict car.

A dismal sight, but it's impossible to think harshly of the Gregs – tonight anyway. They fought like tigers.

The younger children had been taken out, and in the final critical moments an attempt was made to get the women to go. I don't know where Joe Greg was just then, or Mavis, but I did see the struggle with Nell. A group of us were battling to save the detached wash-house and privy, with the bush already catching on the far side of the dwelling. No flames at first, just a blast of hot air whistling up at an acute angle through the tall trees. I saw them flinch, stand still again, and a shower of light debris come floating down, as if they'd merely shaken themselves. A few plumes of smoke curled up from the crisp undergrowth. Below us the entire valley was alight, full of flames and smoke and exploding trees. The din was terrific. Some rural brigade had got down to us, and as they ran a line out their urgent shouts were added to our own pantings and blasphemies. But through it all I heard the raging scream of Nell: "Take your hands off me, you bastards!"

I got a glimpse of her through the swirling smoke, a solid bigboned woman shaking a beater at the sprawling figure of Sam Emerson.

"Where the hell are we to go with eleven kids! This is my home – it's all I've got in the world – by Christ I'll save it ..."

And in a frenzy she threw herself again into the line of men flailing away at the creeping flames below the back verandah.

There, now, is the house, still standing. But amid the black nakedness of earth and human debris it looks wretched in the eerie glow of the burning tree. It lacks the warmth even of lighted windows. Power lines are down everywhere, and the Gregs, like so many others, are back to candle and hurricane lamp. Nobody is in sight as we turn and head up towards the road, but there's a sound of children quarrelling, and the voice of Mavis comes to us clearly in the empty stricken forest: "What's up with you? Everybody else has washed in that dish. You know as well as I do the bloody tanks is empty."

Jim turns his head to give me a tired smile. "They've got a house to sleep in, anyway."

The traffic on the road isn't the unbroken roar that it was some minutes ago, but a lot of vehicles are still going through. No doubt some of the other roads are blocked by fallen trees.

We're beginning to feel the wind again, but that also seems to have weakened. And the air is comparatively clear. There's only a haze, lying among the quiet trees like a morning fog. A newly-arrived volunteer to whom I was talking late in the afternoon told me that there are places in the hills where visibility is better than in Melbourne. He also told me that shipping has been slowed down in the bay since Sunday night, that Moorabbin Airport is closed, and that a leg of the Warrandyte fire got right across to the Maroondah Highway before it was stopped.

For me, anyway, the illusory sense of victory is instantly dispelled as we come on to the road. A police car cruises past with blaring amplifier: "Attention please! Police here – a wide load is following. Drivers please pull in or exercise great care. Attention please ..." 170

"The bull dozer," mutters Jim. We know one has been asked for.

On the far side of the road stands a Shire Council tanker from which men are filling knapsack pumps. A little way behind it is a truck with only the driver in the cabin, sleeping over the wheel. The big white letters on the side of it puzzles me: P.M.C.C. I ask Jim, and 175 he solves it for me – Port Melbourne City Council. I like the idea of the men of Port Melbourne coming up to help us fight fires in the Dandenongs.

Northwards, a few hundred yards away, there is the township itself, the township which has twice been reported as "evacuated". A 180 lot of cars and trucks are about, and there is much coming and going around Blacket's Post Office Store on one side of the road and the Mechanics' Hall on the other. The public telephone box has been closed for two days, during which time Ernie Blacket has never left his post. Only emergency and official calls are being accepted. 185

"Where d'you reckon, Jim?" I ask, because we've come up without any clear idea of where we're going.

He screws up his face. "I've had it, Bob. I've got to get something for me eyes. I can hardly see."

"Home?" Jim lodges with me, and my place is out along Sander's 190 Road.

"How about the Hall? They've got everything there. I'm euchered."

We cross the road in the wake of a big ready-mix concrete transport out of which water is slopping. Before we reach the hall the 195 bull-dozer also goes past. A monstrous piece of equipment mounted on a low-loader, both marked R.A.A.F. It's ironic that when, in a crisis of peace, men call out for the best weapons, they receive the weapons of war. The Country Fire Authority should have things like these. As it is, the Rural Brigades have only bows and arrows. One 200 of them, marked with the name of some obscure township I've never heard of, comes along in the middle of my reflections. A modest little red truck bravely panting up into yet another battle. A three hundred gallon water-tank, a length of hose, some knapsack pumps, and five or six men clinging to the platform at each side. A pitifully 205 inadequate unit to throw into such a holocaust, but they're trained, organised, fearless, and at home in the bush. Time and again in the last few days we've seen the blessed winking red light picking its way in where no vehicle ever went before.

210 Outside the cottage of the Nevinsons their ancient Buick still stands, loaded for instant flight, as it has since Sunday. A mattress and blankets roped to its spacious roof, its interior crammed, except for the driving seat, with boxes and suitcases. These two old people are settling in for another uneasy night. In the weak glow of a kero-
215 sene lamp set on a table we get a glimpse of the moving about in the front room. Small shopkeepers from Prahran, they arrived here only last winter to spend their declining years in the peaceful hills.

It's hot. Oppressively hot. When I look up at the sky I'm surprised to find that all the stars are gone. They were there, however
220 dim, only two hours ago when we raced up York Road from smouldering Montrose. Taken with the high humidity and the falling wind, the discovery excites me. There's that tantalising forecast of a possible thunderstorm. I remark to Jim that it's clouding over, but he doesn't even bother to lift his head.

225 "Might get another dry one," he grunts sceptically. We've had several of them lately, all the fireworks and no rain.

From the higher ground up the road, and looking across the Recreation Reserve, we come in sight of the great glare of the fire over Silvan. A lot of pines have been planted around the dam, and they
230 burn as fiercely as the eucalypts. Lit by the surging flames in colours of grey and yellow and russet-red, clouds of smoke roll majestically up into the black sky. At this distance the silence with which it rages has a subtle terror to us who know all too well the uproar that is going with it. I know every inch of the road from Silvan to Monbulk,
235 and can well imagine what it's like along there now.

West and south-west it seems to be all over. One side of that range was burned out yesterday, the other today. We can't pick out the familiar undulating crest, but the entire face below Kalorama is dotted with glimmering points of light – smouldering trees – like the camp-
240 fires of a bivouaked army.

A lot of people are around the hall as we walk up, including more strangers than ever I've seen in Dogwood before. One animated group is clustered around the tall figure of Vic Chubb, the local policeman. He's in regulation trousers and peaked cap, but no tunic,
245 and is every bit as grimy and red-eyed as the rest of us. Jim stops to speak to a mate, and I hear a woman's hysterical voice

"How do you know? You didn't see – you told me so! Did you *see* her get picked up?"

I recognise her as Mrs. Moran, wife of a postal telegraph worker
250 who lives down behind the Store, and whose home was saved. She's being controlled and comforted by two other women.

"Elsie dear, she's all right, she's all right. Somebody must have taken her out."

"Nobody got burned ..."

"You're only saying that – nobody saw where she went!" She lurches forward. "Mr. Chubb – oh, Mr. Chubb – get them to ask over the wireless. She's only three. She's got a pink frock on – white shoes – she'll be carrying her bride doll ..."

Chubb's been doing a good job. He has an advantage over many other police in that he's bush bred. Jim said he saw him in the thick of it along Ridge Road last night. He looks all-in now, ready to weep from exhaustion – and pity. His articulation, usually crisp and officious, is like that of a man in the early stages of intoxication.

"I've told 'em, I've told 'em. You got nothing to worry about. She's a'right. Somebody's stuffing her with ice-cream somewhere –"

"Ice-cream!" The woman bursts into renewed tears, and her friends drag her away.

Jim's mate curses. "She isn't the only one. If these panic-merchants only knew when to leave alone! They whisk kids off and never think of letting somebody know."

Two men are looking northwards and arguing whether a distant flash was lightning or a speeding car taking a turn in the road. The wind is still in that quarter, but all the violence has gone from it. The long trumpet flowers of a datura growing in the angle of porch and wall give off a sweet smell, overcoming in their immediate vicinity the prevailing odour of smoke. It makes me feel sleepy again, but as we go in we're caught up in a confusion of voices. The dry old hall is buzzing like a beehive.

Some men in the porch are wrangling a familiar bone of contention:

"... can't fight fire on this scale with water."

"Might as well ..." the speaker glances around, grins with relief when he sees we aren't women, but still doesn't finish the sentence.

"Then what the hell are we going to fight it with?"

"Fire! In twenty-six ..."

We push through, and out of earshot.

"Twenty-six me Aunt Fanny!" mutters Jim into my ear. "We can't burn back in an area like this now." He has one hand over his eyes. "Get me into a corner, Bob. Find somebody with a first-aid kit."

How strange it all looks! Candles and hurricane lamps and one pressure lamp. The Mechanics' Hall, traditional social centre of the Australian bush township. Dances, church bazaars, election polling days. Protest meetings: against the Shire Council over a rise in rates, against the Country Roads Board over the state of the highway,

295 against the Board of Works for not laying water on to us. Picture nights, when nothing was quite real except the Little White Hand resting in one's own in the secret darkness.

Relics and familiar features are all here, but they seem fiddling and meaningless on this night of fire. The stack of card tables
300 against the back wall. The Christmas decorations still festooning the dusty rafters. The out-dated billboards, informing us, cajoling us, threatening us. The faithful old piano below the stage.

Tonight it's a refuge, and local headquarters of operations. Some of the trestle tables have been set up, and the forms around all but
305 two of them are full of people, many of them known to me. All are dirty and dishevelled. Some eating and drinking, some quietly talking, some sleeping with heads resting on folded arms. A few, those who have lost their homes, just stare at nothing in particular. They're so used to reading about other people's misfortunes – *has*
310 *this really happened to me?*

Two tables have been reserved for work only, one for the preparation of food and drinks, the other as a first-aid post. Several men are seated at this latter, with their heads resting on an improvised heightened backboard. All have damp cloths over the upper parts of
315 their faces. Along the nearest wall are a few prone figures, the utterly collapsed and the more seriously burned. All the helpers are women and girls.

I take Jim by the arm and steer him over. A Mrs. Shields takes him from me and settles him on the form. She knows both of us.

320 "You can lie on the floor if you like," she tells Jim, "but we're out of pillows. All right like that? Slide down a bit – what d'you think you're going to get, a haircut? Get your head on that board."

Funny, she seems different tonight …

Jim's too lanky to be comfortable, but doesn't want to be fussed
325 over. "I'm apples," he assures her. "It's only me eyes. Got anything to put in 'em?"

I stand by while she puts the drops in and lays a cloth over his eyes.

Jim doesn't want anything else, but I accept a mug of coffee, roll
330 a couple of cigarettes, take a few puffs of Jim's before placing it between his lips, and sit down alongside him.

Some men on the other side of the table are discussing the latest news. I gather that several more lives have been lost during the day, making a total of eight since the fires began. One voice gloomily
335 forecasts a "crown" fire tomorrow if the north wind works up again. "Sherbrooke Forest hasn't been burned out in living memory. If it gets in there it's good-night, nurse."

Two women are kneeling beside a man on the floor who is retching violently into a hand-basin, Mrs. Shields, now dabbing the
blistered foot of a youth sitting beyond Jim, looks at them over her   340
shoulder.

"He's poisoned, that's what I think," she informs them. "Better
get him down to hospital. There's plenty of cars running around."

Yes, she's different. I've only known her as a woman who lives
somewhere up the road, one of the Store gossips, and not usually in-   345
volved in local activities. Tonight she's taken on quite an air of
authority. Perhaps she was a nurse once.

One of the women immediately gets up and goes out. The youth,
his hair damp with perspiration, groans and clutches his stomach.
Another one who's been drinking from a knapsack pump. Rural Bri-   350
gades' equipment is all right, but most of the others pressed into service have been used by the orchardists for insecticides.

Up on the small stage several families are bedding down as best
they can for the night. The children, well aware that stern matters
are in hand, are well-behaved. Some men have just come in carrying   355
mattresses and pillows. They look new, probably part of a donation
from some furnishing store. All kinds of stuff is being rushed up
from the city.

Somebody comes in from the front and says that a lot of soldiers
have just gone up the road: "Six trucks, full to the gills ..."   360

We need equipment far more than we do men, but the news sinks
into me. Perhaps we won 't have to go out again. Perhaps the rain
will come. Jim is fast asleep, the dead cigarette fallen from his slack-
ened lips.

The coffee has brought the sweat out on me again, but it's plea-   365
sant sitting here. And full of interest. I keep thinking: this is how
people behave in a crisis. Voices come at me from all sides. One that
I recognise is telling the story of the big aviation tanker that was sent
up to the Christmas Hills outbreak:

"... and lined it up on a row of fowl-houses that was just begin-   370
ning to burn. Bloke in charge told us it could pump four thousand
gallons in eight minutes. 'Give it a burst!' somebody yells. Stone the
crows, you should have seen them sheds go! Flattened 'em like a
tack. Chooks streaking in all directions – burn or drown ..."

Chuckles, and more voices -   375

"According to the newspapers every bloody township in the
Dandenongs has been evacuated."

"They like that word – evacuated."

"Like they talk about houses exploding."

380   "Fibro-plaster houses *do* explode. The walls don't burn through. The heat keeps building up inside, then off they go – poof!"

"You 're talking about balloons ! What about doors and windows? I saw a couple …"

"It's things in the houses, and round about, that explode. Like cyl–
385 inders of prota-gas and drums of petrol."

"Bill Renton got trapped …"

"Old Ma Stevens – coming up the track with that useless little foxy bitch under one arm and a clucky hen under the other …"

The wagging tongues are beginning to run together, to lose sense
390 and individuality and merge into all the other noises – shuffling feet, clattering dishes, scraping forms, and rumbling wheels out on the road. It's been a long day.

There was the hard-bitten Board of Works man. Two of us left behind to keep watch after the fire had been beaten back at a point
395 where the aqueduct emerges into the open to cross a small depression. He pointed to the blackened and still – smoking concrete pipeline, hung with stalactites of melted bitumen: "We bloody nearly gave 'em a hot-water service in Melbourne, mate!"

It amused me at the time. I begin to shake again now. Somebody
400 standing in front of me puts a hand on my shoulder as I lurch forward, and I look up into the face of Mrs. Shields.

"What's up with you? You're sitting there with a grin on you like a half-stunned duck."

I'm saying something, but I don't know what. She keeps on look-
405 ing at me, curiously.

"Evacuated? What the heck are you talking about?"

"We're still here, aren't we?"

"If I knew where you was getting it from I'd say you was drunk."

True. Mrs, Shields. I'm not drunk. And you're too busy to guess
410 what it is that's tickling me. And that's the whole point of it.

Annotations

2 **weariness**: exhaustion; being very tired – 8 **slope** (n.): a piece of ground or surface that is higher at one end than the other – 9 **knapsack pump** (n.): a water pump carried on the back like a knapsack (= a bag that you carry on your shoulders), for fighting bushfires – 11 **inert** (adj.): not having the strength or power to move – 14 **billy** (n.): (BrE and AustrE), also 'billy can'; a tin pot for cooking or boiling water when you are camping – 18 **gobble** (v.): to eat sth. very quickly or in a way people do not consider polite – 23 **brittle** (adj.): (here) hard and dry – **ground litter**: (here) the leaves and small

branches scattered naturally on the ground; not referring to rubbish left by people – 28 **predicament** (n.): a difficult or unpleasant situation in which you do not know what to do, or you have to make a difficult choice – 35 **roar** (n.): a continuous loud noise, esp. made by a machine or a strong wind – 36 **unceasingly**: continuously – 41 **the northerly**: wind from the north; in this part of Australia that means a hot dry wind – 44 **intimidate**: frighten – 45 **parched**: dried out – **wire grass** (n.): any of various grasses, such as Bermuda grass, that have tough wiry (= slender, but strong in constitution) roots or rhizomes – 48 **fork** (n.): (here) the point of a tree where the division into two or more branches begins – 49 **long-dead veteran**: an old tree – 53 **belch** (v.): to give or send out large amounts of smoke, fire etc. – 55 **thump** (n.): the dull sound that is made when sth. hits a surface – 56 **ridge** (n.): the highest part of a slope, hill, or mountain; the edge – 57 **WATER-TANK**: in this part of Australia at this time the water for drinking and other household uses was collected in water tanks, usu. water that fell as rain on the roof and was then collected in a large metal tank; there was no water delivered through pipes etc. from a central city system – 65 **naked spars**: (here) branches of trees – 66 **rustling**: the sound of dry things, like fallen leaves, moving against each other – 68 **a fury**: (here) energetic, violent activity – 72 **papery** (adj.): (here) dry and thin, like paper – 73 **blighted**: ruined, destroyed – 88 **trudging**: walking with slow, heavy steps, esp. because you are tired – 90 **mate** (n.): (BrE and AustrE) (infml.) used by men as a friendly way to address a man – 91 **stagger** (n.): an unsteady movement of s.o. who is having difficulty in walking – 94 **slurred** (adj.): unclear, inarticulate, blurred – 96 **He's just had it**: he's exhausted – 97 **Ain't**: haven't – 101 **crook** (adj.): (AustrE) (infml.) ill – 102 **getting on for ten**: to be almost ten o'clock – 104 **beater** (n.): a sack that is tied on to the end of a pole; the sack is soaked in water and then the person beats the fire on the ground with the wet sack; very effective, as the portable sack can be taken where water hoses won't reach – 106 **charred** (adj.): burnt black – 107 **novice** (n.): (here) beginner – 111 **higgledy-piggledy**: disorganised, chaotic, messy – 112 **weatherboards**: houses made of horizontal timber panels which are called weatherboards – 115 **piped tree**: a tree which has had the middle burnt out of it so it now resembles a pipe – 119 **dismal** (adj.): unpleasant and sad – 121 **in the final go**: at the last minute – 125 **privy** (n.): (old use) a toilet, esp. one outside a house – 127 **acute angle**: an angle that is less than 90 degree; (here it just means a very steep angle, probably sharper than 90 in the strict maths definition) – **flinch** (v.): to make a sudden small backward movement when you are shocked by pain or afraid of sth. – 128 **debris** (n.): all the pieces that are left after sth. has been destroyed in an accident, explosion, fire, etc. – 131 **din** (n.): a loud unpleasant noise that continues for a long time – 132 **ran a line out**: (here) a hose running out from the fire brigade's truck – 133 **panting**: heavy breathing – 137 **sprawling**: laid out flat on the ground – 141 **in a frenzy**: as if she was mad – **flailing**: beating sth. violently, usu. with a stick – 144 **eerie** (adj.): strange and frightening – 147 **hurricane lamp**: a portable lamp which runs on kerosene; its flame is protected by glass – 150 **stricken**: very badly affected – 151 **tanks is empty**: (sl.) the water tanks are empty – 168 **blaring**: making a loud noise – 172 **SHIRE COUNCIL**: each local area or shire has its own local council to manage public facilities, e.g. water tanks – 186 **reckon** (v.): guess, think – 189 **me**: (sl.) my – 193 **euchered**: (AustrE and NZE) (infml) ruined or exhausted, (here) exhausted – 194 **concrete** (n.): a substance used for building that is made by mixing sand, very small stones, cement, and water – **a big ready mix concrete transport**: usu. it would take cement or concrete around to building sites, now it's being filled with water to fight the fire – 194 **RAAF**: (abbr.) Royal Australian Air Force – 199 **The Country Fire Authority**: the body responsible for fighting bush fires in country areas – 200 **bows and arrows**: (here) primitive weapons; implies the notion of going into modern warfare armed just with bows and arrows – 212 **roped**: tied with a rope – **crammed**: filled as full as possible – 222 **tantalising** (adj.): (here) holding out a promise, like the promise of rain – 225 **another dry one**: a storm with thunder and lightening but no rain (= a dry one with all the fireworks) – 228 **glare** (n.): a bright unpleasant light which hurts your eyes – 229 **SILVAN**: refers to the SILVAN DAM, one of Melbourne's reservoirs for water supply – 231 **russet-red**: a reddish-brown colour – 240 **bivouac**: spend the night outside without tents in a temporary camp – 244 **regulation** (adj.): used or worn because of a rule or custom – **peaked cap**: a cap that has a flat curved part at the front above the eyes; (here) the trousers and cap of his uniform – **no tunic**: without his coat, his uniform jacket – 256 **lurch** (v.): to move suddenly forward – 260 **bush-bred**: he grew up in the bush, he's a local – 263 **like .. intoxication**: (here) as if he's drunk – 265 **a'right**: (colloq.) alright or all right – 268 **panic-merchants**: people who act hastily and thus spread panic – 269 **whisk kids off**: to take kids quickly away from a place – 274 **datura** (n.): any of various chiefly Indian solanaceaous plants of the genus *Datura*, such as the moonflower and thorn apple, having large trumpet-shaped flowers, prickly pods, and narcotic properties – 278 **beehive** (n.): a structure where bees are kept for producing honey – 279 **wrangling**: arguing – 284/285 **then what the hell ... with? "Fire!"**: (here) how can we fight the fire if we don't use water?

Fight the fire with fire, e.g. by burning in a controlled way in front of the fire so it has nothing to burn and will eventually die out – **twenty-six**: 1926 – 286 **out of earshot**: not near enough to hear what s.o. is saying – 287 **Aunt Fanny**: (colloq.) an exclamation meaning "nonsense" – 288 **burn-back**: burn the country around the fire so it can't spread – 291 **pressure lamp**: a kind of portable lamp – 294 **THE COUNTRY ROADS BOARD**: the government body to build and maintain roads – 295 **THE BOARD OF WORKS**: the government body responsible for water, etc. – **not laying water on to us**: not giving us piped water like in the city, hence they have to rely on rainfall and water tanks – 298 **fiddling** (adj.): unimportant, and annoying – 299 **card tables**: folding tables for playing cards on – 301 **rafter** (n.): one of the large sloping pieces of wood that form the structure of a roof – **cajoling**: gradually persuading s.o. to do sth. by being nice, etc. – 304 **trestle table** (n.): a temporary table made of a long board supported on trestles (= two A-shaped frames used as supports for a temporary table) – **forms**: benches to sit on – 306 **dishevelled** (adj.): very untidy – 315 **prone** (adj.): (here) lying down flat – 324 **lanky** (adj.): tall and thin – 325 **I'm apples**: I'm fine – **me**: (sl.) my – **'em** (pron.): (here) short form of "them" – 335 **a "crown" fire**: (probably) a fire in the crown of trees, e.g. a fire that spreads from tree to tree through the high leaves and branches rather than along the ground – 337 **it's good night, nurse**: it's all finished, that would be the end of things – 338 **retching**: trying to vomit – 340 **blister**: a swelling on the skin caused by burns – 352 **orchardist** (n.): s.o. who owns a farm where fruit trees are grown (= an orchard); (here the sentence refers to the fact that the sick young man has drunk water from a pump which was previously used by an orchardist to spray insecticides) – 354 **stern** (adj.): serious – 360 **full to the gills**: very full – 368 **aviation tanker**: a petrol/fuel tanker usu. for aeroplanes but filled with water to fight the fire – 370 **fowl-house**: huts or little houses where chickens are kept – 374 **like a tack**: (here) the sheds were all knocked flat to the ground by the force of the blast of water – **chook** (n.): (infml) (AustrE and NZE) a hen or chicken – 375 **chuckle**: quiet laughter – 380 **fibro-plaster**: prefabricated building material – 385 **prota-gas**: gas for household use in cylinders – 388 **foxy bitch**: a female fox terrier dog – **cluck**: the sound a hen makes – 393 **hard-bitten**: tough – 397 **bitumen** (n.): a sticky substance made from petrol products that is used for making the surface of roads – 406 **What the heck**: (spoken) what the hell, what in heaven's name – 408 **was getting … was drunk**: (sl., bad grammar) were getting … were drunk – 410 **tickling**: amusing

Questions

1   At the beginning of the story, the narrator talks of "one of the most un-real moments I've ever experienced" and a little later of "the most ex-traordinary sensation of loneliness I've ever known." Try to express in your own words what it is that makes him experience these strong, ra-ther strange emotions at this time.

2   Try to locate the region where the story is set by looking at an atlas or map (you will need a map which gives detail for Melbourne and its nearby regions). Can you suggest any reasons why Morrison chose to mention real places, and to give the place names such an important role in his story, rather than just making up a fictional location?

3   In what ways can we see this as a story about "mateship," about the close bonds between men?

4   The story focuses for some time on the story of the Gregs. What role does this episode play in the story?

5   Describe the effects of the fire on the different characters we meet in the story – for example, Vic Chubb or Mrs Shields.

6   Does the narrator see the land as cruel or hostile? How would you de-scribe his relationship to this environment? By searching on the inter-net, see if you can locate some Australian sites with information about bushfires.

7   The end of the story is something of a mystery. Something makes the narrator start laughing; he's so exhausted he almost falls over and Mrs Shields wonders if he's drunk. What do you think it is that makes him laugh to himself in this strange way? What is the "whole point" he men-tions at the very end?

8 | Roderick Finlayson

Roderick Finlayson (1904-1992) was born in Devonport, near Auckland, on the North Island of New Zealand. Growing up around Auckland, he spent his summers working on farms in the Bay of Plenty area, to the south-east of Auckland, developing a close relationship with a Maori family there. Later he lived mainly as a freelance writer. He began writing stories in the early 1930s, wanting to write of the Maori society he had known and also of the destructive effects of Pakeha or European society in New Zealand.

His first collection of stories, *Brown Man's Burden*, appeared in 1938; it includes the story "The Totara Tree." With this collection of stories, Finlayson emerged as the first Pakeha writer to write about Maori culture and society in a way that neither assumed the superiority of European civilisation nor romanticised the Maori character or way of life. His stories do not present a nostalgic view of Maori life but instead show the effects of contact with a European society based on the idea of progress and profit. Finlayson saw Maori culture as having suffered a "gradual invasion ... by modern materialism." In *Brown Man's Burden* he writes of the period between World War I and the Great Depression (1929-1932). In later works he focuses on Maori and Pakeha society in New Zealand during the Great Depression and in World War II.

The Maori community shown in "The Totara Tree" is still a community. However, it is not a community untouched by the coming of European society. It is a small rural "settlement" of people most probably displaced from their original lands. The settlement does not appear to be wealthy. The story recounts a moment of confrontation between Maori and Pakeha values, between the values summed up in the totara tree, which is the old woman's "birth tree" and so "tapu" or sacred, and those suggested by the coming of the new power lines.

But the story does not present a simple fable of good verses evil. We are shown complex variety of attitudes among the Maori. There is a range of opinions about Taranga herself, about whether she really is a "witch" with magical powers or just a mad old woman. The old man, Uncle Tuna, is disgusted by the joking attitude of the younger people. He looks back to the days when proud Maori might still confront the Pakeha in armed struggle. For him the younger people have lost their dignity. The younger man, Panapa, by contrast, supplies the barrel of beer and encourages the partying which eventually leads to a fire and the burning down of a house. Even though Uncle Tuna seems to be the one who is out of touch with the modern world, he is also the one who achieves the final victory for the Maori by advising the others where to bury Taranga.

Perhaps in the contrast between Uncle Tuna and Panapa, Finlayson is suggesting that Maori culture has declined from its noble past because of the destructive influence of European society. But Panapa is also an attractive character. His voice is used to tell much of the story: he's there at the very beginning and at the very end. One of Finlayson's most important achievements in his Maori stories is to find a method for telling the stories as from "inside" the Maori community: the story-teller here seems to be from inside the community closely observing the events as they unfold and understanding the different reactions of the different characters.

While the Maori have a range of different attitudes, they are all drawn close together by the threat represented by the Pakeha. As Lydia Weaver has written in *The Oxford History of New Zealand Literature in English*: "The variety of Maori attitudes to the Pakeha who want to cut down a tapu totara to make way for an electricity pylon suggests that tribal systems are in decay, with a younger generation weary of Uncle Tuna's exploits, and men and women boasting around a barrel of home-brew about what they'll do to the Pakeha. However, there is no sense of the Pakeha inspector and his men as anything but *other*. If Maori resistance degenerates into a rubbish fire and drunken shouting until only the dead old lady is a figure of dignity, the Pakeha, with their red faces and their blustering and their wasted money, have no more dignity and are considerably more alien."

THE TOTARA TREE

People came running from all directions wanting to know what all the fuss was about. "Oho! It's crazy old Taranga perching like a crow in her tree because the Pakeha boss wants his men to cut it down," Panapa explained, enjoying the joke hugely.

"What you say, cut it down? Cut the totara down?" echoed Uncle Tuna, anger and amazement wrinkling yet more his old wrinkled face. "Cut Taranga down first!" he exclaimed. "Everyone knows that totara is Taranga's birth tree."

Uncle Tuna was so old he claimed to remember the day Taranga's father had planted the young tree when the child was born. Nearly one hundred years ago, Uncle Tuna said. But many people doubted that he was quite as old as that. He always boasted so.

"Well it looks like they'll have to cut down both Taranga *and* her tree," chuckled Panapa to the disgust of Uncle Tuna who disapproved of joking about matters of tapu.

"Can't the Pakeha bear the sight of one single tree without reaching for his axe?" Uncle Tuna demanded angrily. "However, this tree is tapu," he added with an air of finality, "so let the Pakeha go cut down his own weeds." Uncle Tuna hated the Pakehas.

"Ae, why do they want to cut down Taranga's tree?" a puzzled woman asked.

"It's the wires," Panapa explained loftily. "The tree's right in the way of the new power wires they're taking up the valley. Ten thousand volts, ehoa! That's power, I tell you! A touch of that to her tail would soon make Taranga spring out of her tree, ehoa," Panapa added with impish delight and a sly dig in the ribs for old Uncle Tuna. The old man simply spat his contempt and stumped away.

"Oho!" gurgled Panapa, "now just look at the big Pakeha boss down below dancing and cursing at mad old Taranga up the tree; and she doesn't know a single word and cares nothing at all!"

And indeed Taranga just sat up there smoking her pipe of evil-smelling torori. Now she turned her head away and spat slowly and deliberately on the ground. Then she fixed her old half-closed eyes on the horizon again. Aue! How those red-faced Pakehas down below there jabbered and shouted! Well, no matter.

Meanwhile a big crowd had collected near the shanty where Taranga lived with her grandson, in front of which grew Taranga's totara tree right on the narrow road that divided the straggling little hillside settlement from the river. Men lounged against old sheds and hung over sagging fences; women squatted in open doorways or strolled along the road with babies in shawls on their backs. The

bolder children even came right up and made marks in the dust on the Inspector's big car with their grubby little fingers. The driver had to say to them, "Hey there, you! Keep away from the car." And
45 they hung their heads and pouted their lips and looked shyly at him with great sombre eyes.

But a minute later the kiddies were jigging with delight behind the Inspector's back. How splendid to see such a show – all the big Pakehas from town turned out to fight mad old Taranga perching in
50 a tree! But she was a witch all right – like her father the tohunga. Maybe she'd just flap her black shawl like wings and give a cackle and turn into a bird and fly away. Or maybe she'd curse the Pakehas, and they'd all wither up like dry sticks before their eyes! Uncle Tuna said she could do even worse than that. However, the older
55 children didn't believe that old witch stuff.

Now as long as the old woman sat unconcernedly smoking up the tree, and the Pakehas down below argued and appealed to her as unsuccessfully as appealing to Fate, the crowd thoroughly enjoyed the joke. But when the Inspector at last lost his temper and
60 shouted to his men to pull the old woman down by force, the humour of the gathering changed. The women in the doorways shouted shrilly. One of them said, "Go away, Pakeha, and bully city folk! We Maoris don't yet insult trees or old women!" The men on the fences began grumbling sullenly, and the younger fellows
65 started to lounge over toward the Pakehas. Taranga's grandson, Taikehu, who had been chopping wood, had a big axe in his hand. Taranga may be mad but after all it was her birth tree. You couldn't just come along and cut down a tree like that. Ae, you could laugh your fill at the old woman perched among the branches like an old black
70 crow, but it wasn't for Pakeha to come talking about pulling her down and destroying her tree. That smart man had better look out.

The Inspector evidently thought so too. He made a sign to dismiss the linesmen who were waiting with ladders and axes and ropes and saws to cut the tree down. Then he got into his big car,
75 tight-lipped with rage. "Hey, look out there, you kids!" the driver shouted. And away went the Pakeha amid a stench of burnt benzine leaving Taranga so far victorious.

"They'll be back tomorrow with the police all right and drag Taranga down by a leg," said Panapa gloatingly. "She'll have no chance
80 with the police. But by golly! I'll laugh to see the first policeman to sample her claws!"

"Oho! they'll be back with sodjers," chanted the kiddies, in great excitement. "They'll come with machine guns and go t-t-t-te at old Taranga, but she'll just swallow the bullets!"

"Shut up, you kids," Panapa commanded.

But somehow the excitement of the besieging of Taranga in her tree had spread like wildfire through the usually sleepy little settlement. The young bloods talked about preparing a hot welcome for the Pakehas tomorrow. Uncle Tuna encouraged them. A pretty state of affairs, he said; if a tapu tree could be desecrated by mere busybodies. The young men of his day knew better how to deal with such affairs. He remembered well how he himself had once tomahawked a Pakeha who broke the tapu of a burial ground. If people had listened to him long ago all the Pakehas would have been put in their place, under the deep sea – shark food! said Uncle Tuna ferociously. But the people were weary of Uncle Tuna's many exploits, and they didn't stop to listen. Even the youngsters nowadays merely remarked "oh yeah?" when the old man harangued them.

Yet already the men were dancing half-humorous hakas around the totara tree. A fat woman with rolling eyes and a long tongue encouraged them. Everyone roared with laughter when she tripped in her long red skirt and fell bouncingly in the road. It was taken for granted now that they would make a night of it. Work was forgotten, and everyone gathered about Taranga's place. Taranga still waited quietly in the tree.

Panapa disappeared as night drew near but he soon returned with a barrel of home-brew on a sledge to enliven the occasion. That warmed things up, and the fun became fast and more furious. They gathered dry scrub and made bonfires to light the scene. They told Taranga not to leave her look-out; and they sent up baskets of food and drink to her; but she wouldn't touch bite nor sup. She alone of all the crows was now calm and dignified. The men were dancing mad hakas armed with axes, knives and old taiahas. Someone kept firing a shot-gun till the cartridges gave out. Panapa's barrel of home-brew was getting low too, and Panapa just sat there propped up against it and laughed and laughed; men and women alike boasted what they'd do with the Pakehas tomorrow. Old Uncle Tuna was disgusted with the whole business though. That was no way to fight the Pakeha, he said; that was the Pakeha's own ruination. He stood up by the meeting house and harangued the mob, but no one listened to him.

The children were screeching with delight and racing around the bonfires like brown demons. They were throwing fire-sticks about here there and everywhere. So it's no wonder the scrub caught fire, and Taikehu's house beside the tree was ablaze before anybody noticed it. Heaven help us! But there was confusion then! Taikehu rushed in to try and save his best clothes. But he only got out with

A Maori protester with the Maori flag in 1995

his old overcoat and a broken gramophone before the flames roared up through the roof. Some men started beating out the scrub with their axes and sticks. Others ran to the river for water. Uncle Tuna capered about urging the men to save the totara tree from the flames. Fancy wasting his breath preaching against the Pakeha, he cried. Trust this senseless generation of Maoris to work their own destruction, he sneered.

It seemed poor old Taranga was forgotten for the moment. Till a woman yelled at Taikehu, "What you doing there with your old rags, you fool? Look alive and get the old woman out of the tree." Then she ran to the tree and called, "Eh there, Taranga! Don't be mad. Come down quick, old mother!"

But Taranga made no move.

Between the woman and Taikehu and some others they got Taranga down. She looked to be still lost in meditation. But she was quite dead.

"Aue! She must have been dead a *long* time – she's quite cold and stiff." Taikehu exclaimed. "So it couldn't be the fright of the fire that killed her."

"Fright!" jeered Uncle Tuna. "I tell you, pothead, a woman who loaded rifles for me under the cannon shells of the Pakeha isn't likely to die of fright at a rubbish fire." He cast a despising glance at the smoking ruins of Taikehu's shanty. "No! but I tell you what she died of," Uncle Tuna continued. "Taranga was just sick to death of you and your Pakeha ways. Sick to death!" The old man spat on the ground and turned his back on Taikehu and Panapa and their companions.

Meanwhile the wind had changed, and the men had beaten out the scrub fire, and the totara tree was saved. The fire and the old woman's strange death and Uncle Tuna's harsh words had sobered everybody by now, and the mood of the gathering changed from its former frenzy to melancholy and a kind of superstitious awe. Already some women had started to wail at the meeting-house where Taranga had been carried. Arrangements would have to be made for the tangi.

"Come here, Taikehu," Uncle Tuna commanded. "I have to show you where you must bury Taranga."

Well, the Inspector had the grace to keep away while the tangi was on. Or rather Sergeant O'Connor, the chief of the local police and a good friend of Taranga's people, advised the Inspector not to meddle until it was over. "A tangi or a wake, it's just as sad and holy," he said. "Now I advise you, don't interfere till they've finished."

But when the Inspector did go out to the settlement afterwards – well! Panapa gloatingly told the story in the pub in town later. "O boy!" he said, "You should have heard what bloody Mr Inspector called Sergeant O'Connor when he found out they'd buried the old
175 woman right under the roots of the bloody tree! I think O'Connor say to him, 'Sure the situation's still unchanged then. Taranga's still in her tree.'"

Well, the power lines were delayed more than ever and in time this strange state of affairs was even mentioned in the House of Parl-
180 iament, and the Maori members declared the Maoris' utter refusal to permit the desecration of burial places, and the Pakeha members all applauded these fine orations. So the Power Board was brought to the pass of having to build a special concrete foundation for the poles in the river bed so that the wires could be carried clear of Taranga's tree.
185 "Oho!" Panapa chuckles, telling the story to strangers who stop to look at the tomb beneath the totara on the roadside. "Taranga dead protects her tree much better than Taranga alive. By golly she cost the Pakeha thousands *and* thousands I guess!"

Annotations

2 **perching**: (here) sitting on a branch high up in a tree – 3 **Pakeha** (n.): (in NZ) (from native Maori language) a person who is not of Maori ancestry, esp. a white person – 12 **boast** (v.): to talk too proudly about your abilities, achievements, or possessions because you want to make other people admire you – 14 **chuckle** (v.): to laugh quietly – 15 **tapu** (adj.): (NZE) (from Maori) sacred; forbidden – 22 **loftily** (adv.): in a supercilious and haughty way; arrogantly – 26 **impish** (adj.): mischievous, roguish – 35 **jabber** (v.): to talk quickly, excitedly, and not very clearly – 38 **straggling**: spreading out untidily in different directions – 40 **sagging**: bending downwards and away from the usual position – 42 **bolder**: more daring – 45 **pout** (v.): to push out your lips because you are annoyed – 47 **jigging**: moving up and down with quick short movements – 53 **wither** (v.): to become drier and smaller and start to die – 63 **MAORI** (n.): s.o. who belongs to the race who first lived in New Zealand – 64 **sullenly** (adv.): in a way of silently showing anger or bad temper – 73 **linesmen** (n.; pl.): people whose job is to take care of railway lines and telephone wires – 76 **stench** (n.): a very strong unpleasant smell – 79 **gloatingly** (adv.): acting in a mode where you show in an unpleasant way that you are happy about your own success or about someone else's failure – 82 **sodjer** (n.): (colloq.) soldier – 83 **go t-t-t-te at old Taranga**: (here) go to shoot at old Taranga – 90 **desecrate**

(v.): to spoil or damage something holy – **busybody** (n.): s.o. who is too interested in other people's private activities – 96 **weary** (adj.): tired of sth. – 98 **harangue**: to address (a person or crowd) in an angry, vehement, or forcefully persuasive way – 99 **haka** (n.): (NZ, Maori) a Maori war chant accompanied by gestures – 111 **sup** (v.): to drink sth., esp. slowly in small amounts – 113 **taiaha** (n.): (NZ; Maori) a carved weapon in the form of a staff, now used in Maori ceremonial oratory – 114 **cartridge** (n.): a metal, cardboard, or plastic tube containing explosive and a bullet that you use in a gun – 115 **propped up**: (here) leaning – 122 **screeching**: making a very unpleasant, high noise with your voice, esp. because you are angry – 131 **caper** (v.): to act or behave playfully; frolic – 147 **pothead** (n.): (infml.) – 168 **meddle** (v.): to deliberately become involved in a situation that does not concern you, or that you do not understand

Questions

1 How does the story place us, as readers, "inside" the Maori community so that we see the Pakeha Inspector and his men as the outsiders?

2 Describe the different values and attitudes of Uncle Tuna and Panapa. What do they share, despite their differences?

3 During the fire, Uncle Tuna reflects: "Trust this senseless generation of Maoris to work their own destruction." What do you think he means by this and how does it link to other elements in this story?

4 Sergeant O'Connor, another policeman, makes a brief appearance in the story with the Inspector. How are his attitudes different from the Inspector's?

5 By searching the Internet or books from your library, find out more about New Zealand's Maori people – their past and their place in present-day New Zealand.

6 A recent novel, also made into a very powerful film, is Alan Duff's *Once Were Warriors*. This story concerns violence and other social problems within contemporary Maori communities in New Zealand's cities. If you can read the novel or see the film try to make comparisons with the situation Finlayson describes, in the 1920s, and the contemporary situation as presented in this more recent story. A new interesting film in that context is for example *The Whale Rider*.

9 | Witi Ihimaera

Witi Ihimaera was born in 1944 in Gisborne on the east cost of New Zealand's North Island. He is widely acknowledged as the first Maori writer to publish both a book of short stories and a novel. He writes in English. His Maori tribal affiliations are described as follows: "He is of Te Aitanga-a-Mahaki descent, with close affiliations to Tuhoe, Te Whanau-a-Apanui, Ngati Kahungunu, and links to Rongowhakaata, Ngati Porou, and Te Whakatohea." This description gives a strong sense of the importance of family and kinship relations in Maori culture. His first collection of stories was *Pounamu, Pounamu* (1972) and his first novel was *Tangi* (1973). These works focussed mainly on Maori rural life. Later work concentrates on urban life and has a stronger political emphasis. Ihimaera has also written about gay experience in *Nights in the Gardens of Spain* (1996).

In 1973 Ihimaera began a career which is perhaps unusual for a writer, in the NZ Ministry of Foreign Affairs, where he remained until 1989. During this period he worked at the NZ High Commission in Canberra and spent four years in New York and Washington, two of them as NZ consul. In 1990 he took up a position as a Lecturer in English at Auckland University.

"The Washerwoman's Children" comes from a collection of short stories published in 1989 called *Dear Miss Mansfield: A Tribute to*

Kathleen Mansfield Beauchamp. Katherine Mansfield (1888 – 1923), as she was known, is New Zealand's best-known writer. She left NZ permanently in 1906 and lived in England and Europe. She mixed with many of the most famous modern writers, but many of her stories recall her own childhood growing up in New Zealand.

In *Dear Miss Mansfield*, Ihimaera writes a series of stories which are like a conversation with Katherine Mansfield. He sees her as a great writer, but he also wants to enter into a dialogue with her from the point of view of modern-day New Zealand and from his own position as a Maori. He writes: "Dear Miss Mansfield, my overwhelming inspiration and purpose comes from my Maori forebears. They are my source as surely as New Zealand was yours. The art of the short story, however, has taken its bearings from your voice also." Of his own stories he writes, "They are stories in themselves, some Maori and some with European themes, recognising the common experiences of mankind."

"The Washerwoman's Children" is related to a famous Mansfield story "The Doll's House" (1922) which is structured around the reactions of various characters to the gift of a doll's house to the children of the Burnell family, a well-off middle-class family. The young girl, Kezia, is contrasted with the other members of her family, for she is the only one who can reach beyond middle-class prejudice as she shares the wonder of the doll's house, especially its miniature lamp, with the children of a poor, socially outcast family, the Kelvey children, Lil and Else, the daughters of a washerwoman. The only words Else speaks are, "I seen the little lamp." The lamp has been seen to "symbolise the potential for transcendence of imposed social values."

In Ihimaera's story, the poor young girl Else has become "Mrs Justice Fairfax-Lawson," a successful judge in England, now retired. She has indeed transcended her poor and disadvantaged beginnings. She is drawn back into her childhood by an invitation to a school reunion back in New Zealand where her sister, now Lilian Bates, still lives. The story traces her reactions as she is forced to remember what was for the most part an unhappy childhood. The story is also structured around a contrast between the two sisters, one who has remained a New Zealander, the other who has turned herself into an Englishwoman, though still a New Zealander as she discovers. Through this comparison, the story explores the values and attitudes of middle-class New Zealand society, values which may appear to be narrow and provincial. At the end of the story, Ihimaera returns us to the famous scene in Mansfield's "The Doll's House" where Else saw the little lamp in the doll's house.

THE WASHERWOMAN'S CHILDREN

Mrs Justice Fairfax-Lawson, sitting in the morning-room of her home at Calverley Park, Tunbridge Wells, received the morning post. Lying on the salver was a brown manila envelope from New Zealand bearing a crest that she had not seen for some fifty years. Despite her usual habit of opening the post before pouring her tea, this letter sat until Penny had cleared. Only then, with a self-directed criticism of "Elspeth, you are being ridiculous," did she lift her letter knife and open the envelope. Inside was a form letter, with blank spaces that had been filled in by hand, as follows:

        45 Jackson Crescent
        Wellington
        New Zealand

        Dear *Elspeth*,
        Your name has been referred to the Karori Primary
        School Anniversary Committee by *your sister, Lilian
        Bates*.
            The Committee, which has been actively working to-
        wards the centennial celebrations of the School, would
        like to extend to you a warm invitation to attend an An-
        niversary Dinner in the school hall on 10 August this
        year, at 7.30 p.m. Roll Call, by year, will be taken at 5
        p.m. A photographer will record the happy event. The
        Committee hopes you will be able to come along.

        Yours sincerely
        (Mrs) Lena Holmes

The letter was perforated with a tear-off portion bearing the address of the committee and, "I will be able/unable to attend: I attended Karori Primary School from … . to … . My registration fee of $20 is/ is not enclosed."

Mrs Justice Fairfax-Lawson was somewhat nonplussed. The use of her Christian name by a person whom she did not know, called Lena Holmes, irritated her. But most of all the letter brought memories of school days which she hoped had faded forever. Bearing in mind the time difference between England and New Zealand, she

telephoned her sister in Wellington. "Lilian, dear? *What* is going ₃₅
on?"

Given her initial reaction to the invitation, Mrs Justice Fairfax-
Lawson was amused to find herself, three months later, sitting in the
third row of the Business Class section of an Air New Zealand flight
from Gatwick to Los Angeles en route for Auckland. Not only that, ₄₀
but no sooner had she seated herself than the purser, on the advice
of the ground staff who had recognised her, invited her to take a seat
in First Class. Her sense of gratification was only undercut by the
fact that the passenger seated next to her, when told that she "was in
the judiciary", assumed she was a typist or else the wife of a judge ₄₅
(she was not the sort to be mistaken for a mistress); silly pompous
little man. Luckily there was a window seat vacant three rows ahead
and Mrs Justice Fairfax-Lawson firmly invited her neighbour to take
it. Once that was achieved she took up her Dorothy Sayers, but only
briefly before setting it to one side and watching England sinking ₅₀
beneath her.

If anybody had been looking at Mrs Justice Fairfax-Lawson, they
would have seen a slim and elegant woman of pleasant good looks
and a fresh English rose complexion. They would certainly not have
guessed from her appearance, or even any intonation of voice or ₅₅
physical mannerism, that she had actually been born and raised in
New Zealand. There was not a shred of the Antipodean about her,
nor any of the hallmarks of the Antipodean Woman Abroad – the
tightly curled perm, twinset and pearls and bright magpie look
which characterised all New Zealanders south of Balmoral. Instead, ₆₀
what any other passenger would have seen was exactly what Mrs
Justice Fairfax-Lawson had become – a romantic Englishwoman, in
her prime, knowing exactly where she is because she can remember
quite clearly exactly how far she has travelled – and Mrs Justice
Fairfax-Lawson had travelled a very long way indeed. Home Coun- ₆₅
ties style had always meant so much to her that being taken for English was quite a compliment and logical enough. All the same, there
was a sense of fairness in Mrs Justice Fairfax-Lawson which allowed
her to accept that her country of birth would want to claim her – as
it was prone to do, given her successes – as one of its very own. As a ₇₀
judge, Mrs Justice Fairfax-Lawson well knew that all *known* facts
must be taken into account when any case came before the bench
and, if she was trying herself for identification, she would have to
weigh against the fact that although she was British by virtue of her
marriage to the late Hon. Rupert Fairfax-Lawson, she had neverthe- ₇₅
less maintained dual citizenship with the country of her birth. Much
as she disliked the idea of balancing on both sides of the scales, Mrs

Justice Fairfax-Lawson had to admit that giving up *anything* at all had always been difficult for her. Add to this that all her side of the
80 family obstinately remained in New Zealand and that they were her *only* family (she and the Hon. Rupert Fairfax-Lawson being childless and not at all pleased with the Hon. Rupert Fairfax-Lawson's scurrilous nephews), and one realised the depth of her dilemma. She was as much a New Zealander because her family made her one. She
85 could not escape them – and nor would she want to – because she loved them; yes, *loved* was not too strong a word. And she did so with familial pride and devotion, particularly her elder sister Lilian, who had become a grandmother again. So it was a *fait accompli* really, with the gavel confirming the decision and dismissing the
90 court.

Mrs Justice Fairfax-Lawson was about to resume her Dorothy Sayers, but by that time champagne and caviar were being served. Not long after that, dinner – either roast duck or lamb – was offered. Bearing in mind the long journey ahead, Mrs Justice Fairfax-Lawson
95 therefore decided to nap rather than to read. Eight hours later, after more champagne and more roast duck, her flight landed at Los Angeles. Shortly thereafter she was on her way again, with fourteen hours of flying time ahead and the vast expanse of the South Pacific below, bound for Auckland and thence Wellington, New Zealand.

100 Lilian Bates was waiting with her husband George at the Domestic Terminal. There was, at close inspection, a family resemblance to her younger sister Elspeth, but no one would ever have taken Lilian for anything but a New Zealander – at a pinch, an Australian perhaps – and that was where the likeness ended. Lilian's cheeks were
105 ruddy, whereas her sister's were pallid, and Lilian's spontaneity expressed itself in its overeagerness and anxiousness, whereas Elspeth's was under control, *quite.* Apart from that, years of healthy living and appetite had turned Lilian's figure to pear-shaped, whereas Elspeth was still, as ever, a wishbone. Somewhere far back
110 in their lives there had been a parting of the ways. In Elspeth's case it had been the winning of a major scholarship to Cambridge when she was nineteen. As for Lilian, her fate had been forever sealed when George Bates, then garage mechanic and now proprietor of Bates Towaway Trucks, admiring her lines, cast an eye over her, ran
115 her round the block a couple of times, found her bodywork in good condition and pronounced, "She'll do."

"Now, George, don't forget," Lilian told him. "She likes to be called Elspeth. Not Elsie. Or Ellie. Or Else. Or anything but Elspeth." She picked at his tie. "The way you go on," George replied,
120 "you'd think she was the bloody Queen of England." Lilian gri-

maced as if she had never heard such words from his lips before. "And keep your bloodys to your trucks, George – or save them up for when it's just us." George rolled his eyes and Lilian tried to hug him around. "Oh please, George, *do* behave. You know I haven't seen Elspeth for six years now. That's such a long time. She's my only sister after all and – Oh, there she is! Oh, George" – Lilian broke away from him and began to run toward the woman who had just come through the gate. George had always known that his wife was a real softie, but her abrupt emotional departure surprised him. *Why, they're as different as chalk to cheese*, he thought. He watched as Lilian flung her arms around her sister and wept on her shoulder – he hadn't realised that Lilian would be so affected. He felt a lump in his throat at the sight of these two middle-aged women embracing like this – Lilian, as always, so open with her emotions, and *Elspeth* as gracious as ever – you'd think she was waving from a bloody Rolls. He walked over to them. Elspeth said, "Why, George!" in that cultured voice of hers and proffered a cheek for him to kiss. And Lilian stepped aside, saying, "It's really her, George, she's really here," as if he couldn't see that for himself.

Mrs Justice Fairfax-Lawson had planned to stay in New Zealand for three weeks but had not expected that her sister would want to make the most of it. She should have realised when they arrived at the house and were greeted by Lilian's two daughters and their children – plus the new baby – that she would be kept busy it was understandable, she supposed, that Lilian would want to have dinner on the first evening for "Just us and the family" – but when confronted with the cheery barbecue that evening and guests including the local mayor, she knew that life was not going to be that simple. Over that first week Lilian would alternate between expression of "Oh, you must still be jet-lagged, Elspeth. Why don't you go up to the bedroom and rest?" and frequent trips to answer the front doorbell with, "Why, hello!" to yet more neighbours bearing yet more platefuls of lamingtons, pikelets or scones. Nor could the visits possibly be accidental, despite protestations that "We just dropped by" – Oh no, these ladies in their cardies and pearls had just been to the local hairdressing salon, and once ensconced in Lilian's sitting-room with a cuppa, were there to *stay*. Even the innocent "I'm just popping down to the shop, Elspeth. Why not come for a ride?" would turn into a virtual royal procession throughout the land. And at each house the hostess would be ready and waiting with "Why, Lilian, do come in! And this is your sister, isn't it! Elspeth? Lilian has told us so much about you. You're just in time for a cuppa tea –" before opening the door wider and turning to others gathered inside –

"isn't she, ladies!" These ladies knew that New Zealand hospitality
165 was the best in the world, and they weren't going to let the side
down – especially with such a famous person in their midst. And so
the polite conversation would begin, with everybody minding their
p's and q's and trying not to be too colonial – clinking the teacups
ever so softly and not dropping one crumb of the lamingtons – until,
170 with a little squeak of a cough, the hostess would turn to Mrs Justice
Fairfax-Lawson and ask, "So you live in England, do you?" Where-
upon all tea-drinking would be suspended as Mrs Justice Fairfax-
Lawson, as custom required, told them about life as it was lived by
those whose Title and Reputation enabled an English Existence
175 spread between an apartment in Westminster and a country home in
Tunbridge Wells. On her part, Mrs Justice Fairfax-Lawson knew that
she, too, couldn't let the side down – her side being her sister – and
she rose to every occasion. For despite her caustic tongue, Mrs Justice Fairfax-Lawson would not have hurt her sister for anything in
180 the world. And success was measured by the indrawn gasps of
"You don't *say*!," "Listen to *that*, Millie!", "How *interesting*!" and
"Do go on." And if, near the end of the socialising, the hostess
sighed, "Oh, it sounds so different from life here," then Mrs Justice
Fairfax-Lawson knew also that form required her to offer general-
185 ities like "But you are so lucky, New Zealand is such a paradise, it is
so green, and your food is so delicious" – even if she didn't really
mean it herself. Then Lilian would drive her sister home, and Mrs
Justice Fairfax-Lawson would go up to her bedroom and have a lie-
down and listen to Lilian's happy voice downstairs as she re-
190 sponded to telephone calls from the friends just visited – "Oh yes,
I'll tell her! Yes, we are all very proud of her! No, *really*, do you really
think we are that alike?" Such things had always been important to
Lilian.

However, when, at the beginning of the second week, Mrs Justice
195 Fairfax-Lawson came across her photograph on page seven of the
Dominion and read the accompanying article she became most dis-
pleased. It wasn't really the photograph, which was at the very *least*
twenty years old – and while Mrs Justice Fairfax-Lawson was as
vain as the next person, a photograph of that vintage could only
200 draw unhappy comparisons with one's current estate – nor was it
the article itself, which was succinct and to the point:

> Mrs Justice Elspeth Fairfax-Lawson, M.B.E., (pictured right) returned last
> week for a private visit to New Zealand, her first in six years. Mrs Fair-
> fax-Lawson recently retired from the U.K. judiciary following the death
205 > of her husband, the late Hon. Rupert Fairfax-Lawson, M.P. Born in Well-
> ington in 1910, Mrs Fairfax- Lawson will be well known to New Zealan-

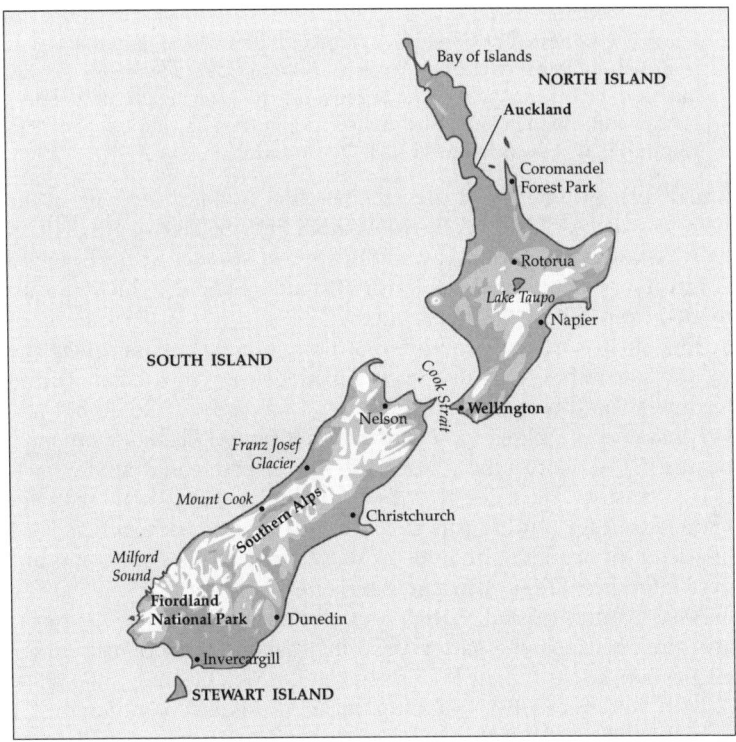

New Zealand, North and South Islands

ders as the founder and first chairperson of the Wellington Women's Co-
operative. Educated at Cambridge, England, Mrs Fairfax-Lawson served
in British Intelligence during the Second World War, where she met her
husband. Following the war she began a private legal practice in London,
Fairfax and Madden, and was invited to join the U.K. judiciary in 1962.
Her M.B.E. was awarded by H.R.H. Queen Elizabeth II in 1970.

The displeasure stemmed from the headline and last sentence of the
text, to wit: FAMOUS NZER RETURNS FOR SCHOOL REUNION
and "Mrs Justice Fairfax Lawson is a guest speaker at next week's
Anniversary Dinner of the Karori Primary School, which she attended from 1915 to 1923."

Mrs Justice Fairfax-Lawson was therefore *very* cross when she
went down to breakfast that morning and, seeing this, Lilian said to
George, "You'd best leave us a minute, George dear." To do her justice, Lilian was looking very contrite. She poured Elspeth a hot cuppa and, "The photo's nice," she said. But Elspeth could not be paci-
fied so easily. "How could you *do* this, Lilian. You *know* that my
main reason for coming was to see you, and that I have only agreed
to attend the school reunion because *you* want to go. I am going under sufferance, Lilian. You know how much I *hated* that school. The
way the parents treated Mother and vilified Father was so unspeak-
able. Just because she had to take in washing and because father
was a bankrupt." Lilian bit her lip and, "Yes, Elspeth," she said.
"Can't you remember anything at all?" Elspeth continued. "It
wasn't Mother's fault that she had to send us to school in dresses
made from bits given her by other people – other people's cast-offs
and curtain material – but did the other children understand? No,
they *didn't.*" Whenever Lilian was embarrassed, her face took on a
silly shamefaced smile, and, "You're quite right, Elspeth," she said,
her heart aching from the pain of the reprimand. *And a vivid picture
flashed into her mind of Lena Logan sliding, gliding, dragging one foot,
giggling behind her hand, shrilling, "Is it true you're going to be a servant
when you grow up, Lil Kelvey?" And taunting her again with "Yah, yer
father's in prison!" before running away giggling with the other girls.* "We
were *always* on the outside," Elspeth said. "They never invited us to
play in any of their games, because we weren't good enough for
them. And *now* I read in the newspaper that I am to be guest
speaker –" Lilian folded her hands in her lap and looked down and,
"They only want you to say a few words," she said. "A few words?"
Elspeth cried. "That's more than they deserve. There was only one
girl, just *one*, who ever showed us a kindness and –"

Lilian couldn't take any more. Her silly smile opened too wide
and let the tears through. She tried to say something to Elspeth,

gulped and instead patted Elspeth on the hand and kissed her right 250
cheek. Then she stood up and left the table. Elspeth, still furious, sat
there in the grip of her own recollections and how, it seemed, she
had only managed to survive by holding on with a piece of Lil's
skirt screwed up in her hand, holding on all day, *every* day, holding
on so tight, so *tight*. And not saying a word to anybody but wanting 255
to scream, just *scream*, with the loneliness and pain and awfulness of
it all. Then Elspeth heard George and looked up into his disapproving face. "You were too hard on her, Elspeth," he said. "Lilian may
be the elder of the two of you but she's the one who suffers more.
You should have a care for your sister. She thinks the bloody world 260
of you." And that only made Elspeth feel worse – about her petulance and, oh, at Lilian too for being such a *martyr* and running off
like that! You'd think they were still children the way Lilian be-
haved – going off so bravely to sulk like that and make her feel so
mean. Elspeth looked at George and sighed. He indicated the direc- 265
tion in which Lilian had gone.

"Lilian? Lilian," Elspeth called. She heard Lilian reply, "In here,
dear," and found her at a small card table in the lounge. Lilian had
put on her reading glasses and was cutting the article about Elspeth
out of the newspaper. "What *are* you doing?" Elspeth asked. She 270
came up behind Lilian and looked over Lilian's shoulder. On the
card table was a large scrapbook. Elspeth recognised it instantly – it
was the book their mother had begun when her daughters had both
started school and filled year by year with school reports, handwrit-
ten memories, school magazine photographs, newspaper clippings: 275
ELSPETH KELVEY IS DUX OF SCHOOL; LOCAL GIRL WINS
CAMBRIDGE SCHOLARSHIP; MORE HONOURS FOR KELVEY;
OUR ELSPETH TOPS CLASS AT CAMBRIDGE; ENGAGEMENT
OF ELSPETH KELVEY TO SON OF LORD FAIRFAX-LAWSON -
and other memorabilia. Elspeth gave a small cry and reached over 280
to leaf through the pages: LOCAL PERSONALITY AWARDED
M.B.E.; FAIRFAIX-LAWSON RETIRES FROM U.K. JUDICIARY .
"It's mostly all about you," Lillian said softly. "I never did much
myself except marry George and have my two girls. But oh, Mother
was so proud of you, Else, love. You wouldn't believe the times she 285
would go through this scrapbook. 'Look at our Else,' she used to say.
'All those brains, where'd they come from!'" The mood sweetened
between the two sisters, and Elspeth reached over and put her hand
in Lilian. "Anyway," Lilian said, "when Mother died I kept the
scrapbook going. I don't know why really. It would have been a 290
shame to just let it go, don't you think?" And suddenly Lilian
started to weep again, saying, "I'm so sorry, Else, I just didn't

realise –" And Elspeth replied, "Come, come, Lilian. Oh, Lilian, *do*
stop" – because she had begun to recall how difficult it had all been
295 for Mother and Lilian to keep her at school. "Oh, Lilian!" she said,
furious, because tears were so unseemly at their age.

Afterwards Elspeth told Lilian that she had better check with the
Karori Centenary Committee how many words a "few" constituted.
They had a cuppa tea and laughed about the absurdity of two
300 grown women losing control like that. "There was never a jealous
bone in your body, was there?" Elspeth asked her sister. "A couple
of times," Lilian admitted. Elspeth smiled and turned away, intend-
ing to go up to her bedroom. Just as she went through the door, Lilian called to her. "Oh, Elspeth," she said. Elspeth turned and,
305 "Yes?" she asked; Lilian's attitude was resolute and firm. "Although
we may have been a washerwoman's children," she said, "we were
never too proud" – which was as just the sort of infuriating commonplace thing Lilian always liked to say.

And after all that, not to mention the effort that Elspeth had put
310 into preparing a ten-minute address, Lilian came down with a bad
flu on the very night of the dinner. "You will get up this instant," Elspeth ordered. "Put on your pearls and come with me. Her tone was
similar to that she used when addressing felons from the Bench. Lilian nodded and tried but, "Oh, Elsbed, I don'd thig I cad," she said.
315 "You bedder go wib Geord. Geord? You go wib Elsbed to the didder." Lilian reached for a handkerchief. George, taken by surprise,
said, "Go back to school? Not on your bloody life." Then Elspeth interrupted him, saying, "Lilian Kelvey, it is already after five. You are
as strong as a horse and *never* get the flu. Get up at once." But it was
320 obvious that no command would work. "Oh, by dose," Lilian said,
blowing on it. "By hed," she said, holding it. "Elsbed, you should
rig the cobbidee and ask theb to ged sobody to pig you ub." And
that was that – which explains how Mrs Justice Fairfax-Lawson was
delivered, an hour late, by a nice but obviously awestruck Maori
325 committee member called Mrs Maraki.

No sooner had Mrs Justice Fairfax-Lawson walked through the
door of the crowded Assembly Hall than she saw a woman gasp
and whisper behind her hand to her companion, and then *sliding,
gliding; dragging one foot and shrilling* she came, calling, "Elspeth! Yoo
330 hoo, Elspeth! And Mrs Justice Fairfax-Lawson reeled backward as if
she had been hit, and reached out for Lil's hand and to hold a piece
of Lil's skirt. "Elspeth?" the woman laughed. "You must remember
me! I'm Lena Holmes! See?" She pointed rather superfluously at a
small tag on her dress with her name and CHAIRMAN ANNIVER-
335 SARY COMMITTEE written on it. "I used to be Lena Logan. Re-

member? You and I were in the same class. But you were much younger of course. Come along with me." Proudly, Lena Holmes took Mrs Justice Fairfax-Lawson's arm and began to steer her possessively in the direction of other committee members. *Yah, yer father's in prison.* "Cora? May I introduce Elspeth to you? But you know her of course. Weren't you in Mrs Fredericks' class together? Oh, you will have some stories to tell! And this is Peggy, Elspeth. Peggy used to be the horrid little girl who did ballet – oh, we hated her, didn't we! And you can remember Annabelle? Her aunt was the postmistress. Oh, you *must* remember Miss Leckey and that terrible hat she used to wear!" *Oh yes. I remember. When Miss Leckey had no further use for it, she gave it to Mother. Lilian used to wear it.* "We are so sorry, Elspeth, to hear that Lillian won't be able to come. What a shame. Never mind, you are in good hands now. We'll look after you, won't we ladies!" *Yes, you'll all run after me and make fun of me and sneer and laugh and wrinkle your noses as I pass and –*

"Are you all right, Elspeth?" The voice sounded so loud in her ear that Mrs Justice Fairfax-Lawson was startled. Lena Holmes was looking at her, concernedly. "Oh. Yes," Mrs Justice Fairfax-Lawson said. "The trip. The strain." Lena Holmes nodded. "I do hope you aren't catching your sister's flu. There's a lot of it going around," she said. "But come along, we must get you tagged!" She laughed as she took Mrs Justice Fairfax-Lawson's hand. *Yah, yah, your mother washes clothes and your father's a jailbird.* "There!" Lena Holmes cried as she branded Mrs Justice Fairfax-Lawson with a label, ELSIE KELVEY, so that everybody – everybody – could remember that awful little girl with cropped hair, remember ladies? *That's her, over* there.

Suddenly a hand bell began to ring. A middle-aged man who could *never* have been young was standing in the centre of the hall, swinging the bell to and fro. His face was red with mirth as the bell clanged and boomed and shattered the conversation. Lena Holmes put her hands to her ears and said, "Oh, that Johnny Johnston! Isn't he a one?" One of the other men ran out to wrestle with "Johnny" and the crowd watched and grinned with amusement – Wasn't this fun? That Johnny, he *never* changed, good old Johnny. And all of a sudden Johnny was running between people, trying to escape his friend, and the women gave little screams and the men pretended to scrimmage and then he was heading for Mrs Justice Fairfax-Lawson and the shock of recognition spread over his face as, pointing at her, he said, "I know you! You're you're –" *Yes. My name is Elsie. My sister is Lil. My mother washes your mother's clothes. You are a horrid boy.* But before he could say anything more he was tackled and down he went. And Lena Holmes, pretending to be a little girl, went over to

the two men lying on the floor, wagged a little finger and said in a
squeaky voice, "Bad boys. Bad boys. I'm going to tell Mrs Fredericks
on you!" What a laugh that caused – that Lena Logan, the same as
ever. Then Lena Holmes laughed herself and clapped her hands,
clap, clap, CLAP. "Roll call, everybody! Roll call! Everybodeeee,"
and she led the way to the English Room, where the group photograph was to be taken.

Mrs Justice Fairfax-Lawson closed her eyes and took a deep
breath. *Pull yourself together*, she said to herself. The shock, the
crowd, the smell of chalk, the bonhomie, all these people acting like
children, pretending that school had been such fun and they were
all friends. Whereas she had only had one friendly gesture made toward her. *Stop it, Elspeth.* For who was she to make such assump-
tions? *STOP IT.* Feeling better, Mrs Justice Fairfax-Lawson joined the
others. She smiled at everybody and was as charming as they expected her to be. She laughed just like everybody else at the photo-
grapher's frantic attempts to arrange the "children" according to
height, and when she had to say CHEEEESE she did so as long as
the rest did until the flashbulb popped. But deep inside her the little
girl she once was still cringed and sought for a piece of dress to hold
on to.

The bell rang again, far away, to announce that dinner would
soon be served. Well-wishers approached Mrs Justice Fairfax-Lawson to say, "We are so looking forward to hearing you speak," or,
"We are so delighted that you will be speaking on our behalf as fellow pupils of the school," and she was so surprised, absolutely *over-
whelmed*, by the warmth of it all. And she realised that the address
she *was* going to give would be too pompous and too serious, for
these returned pupils wished only for companionship and good
memories and wonderful tributes to friends and school. And she
heard Lilian's voice in her mind saying, *We were never too proud, Elspeth, never too proud.*

So that when, following the dinner in the hall, it was time for Mrs
Justice Fairfax-Lawson to rise and speak, she had to pause and re-
consider her words. The hall looked so gay and colourful, with
streamers hanging from the ceiling and flowers arranged on the
trestles and food – jellies, pavlovas, salads, lamingtons – sparkling
on the tables. And there were all those ridiculous elderly people, sitting on forms, faces gazing up at hers in expectation. And it came to
her just what she should say. "Ladies and gentlemen," she began.
"Boys and girls," and everybody laughed. "Like you all, I attended
this school with my sister. There was once a little girl and her sisters
who came to school one day and told us all about a wonderful gift –

a doll's house." To one side Elspeth heard Lena Holmes gasp with
pleasure. "Inside was a little lamp." Mrs Justice Fairfax-Lawson
paused at the memory. *You can come and see our doll's house if you
want to, said Kezia. Come on. Nobody's looking.* "I think that girl died   425
some years ago but what she did stands as a shining symbol to all of
us. Certainly it became a symbol for me." The silence was such that
a dropped pin could have been heard. "Although my sister and I
were the children of a washerwoman" – *There, it was out* – "that girl
showed us the little lamp. I have never forgotten that lamp, ever. Its   430
flame has been a constant inspiration to me to always reach out –
like that girl did – to others. To extend myself, become a better person and perhaps make the world a better place to live in. Were it not
for that kindness, or similar kindnesses which I'm sure you all remember being done to you at this school, none of us would have be-   435
come the people we are today. I would not have become the person
I have."

Mrs Justice Fairfax-Lawson had to pause again. *I seen the little
lamp, she said softly.* She went to resume but somebody had begun to
clap and very soon that person was followed by another and an-   440
other, until the whole hall was on its feet and clapping at the memory of a school-friend, now gone, who had been so important in all
their lives. And as they did so, Mrs Justice Fairfax-Lawson smiled a
rare smile and thought to herself that what she had said was just the
silly commonplace sort of thing that Lilian would have liked.   445

Annotations

3 **salver** (n.): a large metal plate used for serving food or drink at a
formal meal – **manila** (n.): strong brown paper used for making en-
velopes – 4 **crest** (n.): a special picture used as a sign of a family,
town, school etc. – 18 **centennial**: the day or year exactly 100 years
after a particular event – 21 **roll call** (n.): the act of reading out an official list of names to check who is there – 30 **nonplussed** (adj.):
stunned – 41 **purser** (n.): a senior flight attendant who is also in
charge of the cabin crew on an airplane – 45 **judiciary** (n.): (fml.) all
the judges in a country who, as a group, form part of the system of
government – 56 **mannerism** (n.): a way of speaking or moving that
is typical of a particular person – 57 **shred** (n.): a very small amount
– **Antipodean**: (often humorous) s.o. from Australia or New Zealand
– 59 **magpie** (n.): a bird with black and white feathers and a long tail
– 75 **Hon.**: the written abbrev. of honourable (1), used in the titles of
British nobles, judges and Members of Parliament – 80 **obstinately**
(adv.): persistently – 82 **scurrilous** (adj.): libellous, (here) deceiving –

89 **gavel** (n.): a small hammer that the person in charge of a meeting, law court, auction etc. hits on a table in order to get people's attention – 103 **at a pinch**: if necessary in a particularly difficult or urgent situation – 105 **ruddy** (adj.): sth. looks pink and healthy – **pallid** (adj.): unusually or unhealthily pale – 109 **wishbone** (n.): the breast bone from a cooked chicken etc., which two people pull apart to decide who will make a wish – 137 **proffer** (v.): offer – 152 **cuppa** (n.): (spoken BrE) a hot cup of tea – **popping**: going there quickly – 153 **lamington** (n.): (in Australia and NZ) a cube of sponge cake coated in chocolate and dried coconut – **pikelet** (n.): a dialect word for "crumpet" (= a small round bread with holes in one side, eaten hot with butter) – **scone** (n.): a small round, soft cake sometimes containing dried fruit – 155 **cardie** (n.): (also "cardy") (infml.) short for "cardigan" – 156 **ensconce** (v.): to put yourself in a comfortable and safe place – 152 **cuppa** (n.): (spoken BrE) a hot cup of tea – **popping**: going there quickly – 180 **indrawn** (adj.): drawn or pulled in – 201 **succinct** (adj.): clearly expressed in a few words – 221 **contrite** (adj.): remorseful; feeling guilty and sorry for something bad that you have done – 225 **going under sufferance**: going with reluctance and the capacity to endure pain – 227 **vilify** (v.): to say bad things about s.o., esp. things that are not true, in order to influence other people against them – 231 **bit** (n.): a piece of sth. larger – 232 **cast-offs** (n.): clothes that you do not wear any more and give to s.o. else – 236 **reprimand** (n.): rebuke, strong criticism – 239 **yer**: used in writing as an infml. way of saying "your" – 261 **petulance** (n.): annoying or childish impatience – 264 **sulk** (v.): to show that you are annoyed about sth. by being silent and having an unhappy expression on your face – 272 **scrapbook** (n.): a book with empty pages where you can stick pictures, newspaper articles, or other things you want to keep – 307 **infuriating** (adj.): very annoying – 313 **felon** (n.): s.o. who is guilty of a serious crime – 314 **Oh, Elsbed, ... cad**: Oh, Elsbed (This spelling reflects the fact that Lilian has a heavy cold.), I don't think I could – 315 **You bedder ... the didder**: You better go with George. George? You go with Elsbeth to the dinner' – 322 **rig ... ub**: (dial.) ring the committee up and ask if they get somebody to pick you up – 324 **awestruck** (adj.): feeling extremely impressed by the importance, difficulty, or seriousness of s.o. or sth. – 330 **reel**: to step backwards suddenly and almost fall over, esp. after being hit or getting a shock – 338 **to steer** (v.): to guide s.o. to a place, esp. by putting your hand on their back, shoulder etc. and gently pushing them – 345 **postmistress** (n.): a woman who is in charge of a post office – 351 **sneer** (v.): to smile or speak in a very unkind way – 355 **strain** (n.): stress – 359 **jailbird** (n.): (infml.) s.o. who has spent a lot of time

in prison – 362 **cropped** (adj.): cut short – 365 **mirth** (n.): happiness and laughter – 366 **clang** (v.): making a loud ringing sound – 373 **scrimmage** (n.): (infml.) a fight – 379 **wag** (v.): (here) to shake your finger repeatedly to show disapproval – 383 **roll call**: the act of reading out an official list of names to check who is there – 388 **bonhomie** (n.): (from French, esp. literary term) a friendly feeling among a group of people – 414 **streamer** (n.): a long narrow piece of coloured paper, used for decoration at special occasion – 415 **jelly** (n.): a soft solid substance made with sweetened fruit juice and gelatine – **pavlova** (n.): a light cake made of meringue, cream, and fruit

Questions

1 Read Katherine Mansfield's story "The Doll's House" alongside "The Washerwoman's Children." In what ways has Ihimaera developed the meaning of Mansfield's story?

2 Try to note how your reactions to the two sisters changes throughout the story. Describe in your own words the differences between the two sisters.

3 How would you describe the author's attitudes to NZ society? Is he critical? Does the story use satire? Does he suggests any positive aspects in that society?

4 Read the final two paragraphs of the story. At the very end, Elspeth describes her speech as "just the sort of silly commonplace sort of thing that Lilian would have liked." This seems to dismiss what she has just said to the audience, even though there seems to be deep emotion in her own memories of being shown the doll's house. Write down your feelings about this conclusion.

ABBREVIATIONS

abbr.	= abbreviation	l.	= line
adj.	= adjective	ll.	= lines
adv.	= adverb	lit.	= literary/ily
Abor.	= Aborginal language; indigenous language	n.	= noun
		p.	= page
AustrE	= Australian English	pp.	= pages
BrE	= British English	pl.	= plural
NZE	= New Zealand English	prep.	= preposition
derog.	= derogative	sing.	= singular
e.g.	= *exempli gratia*; for example	sl.	= slang
		s.o.	= someone
etc.	= *et cetera*; and so on	s.th.	= something
esp.	= especial(ly)	U.S.	= United States
infml.	= informal(ly)	usu.	= usual(ly)
interj.	= interjection	v.	= verb

ACKNOWLEDGEMENTS

Texts

The texts in this collection still under copyright have been reprinted within the terms of §46 URG via the clearing agency VG WORT. The sources are as follows:

Page 38: Thea Astley, *Heart is Where the Home Is*, from: Thea Astley *It`s raining in Mango*, Penguin Books, Ringwood, Victoria, Australia, 1989.

Page 51: David Malouf, *Blacksoil Country*, from: David Malouf *Dream Stuff*, pp. 116 – 130, Chatto Windus, London, 2000.

Page 67: Gerald Murnane, *Land Deal*, from: Gerald Murnane *Velvet Waters*, McPhee Gribble, Ringwood, Victoria, Australia, 1990.

Page 74: Lily Bret, *The Holiday*, from: Lily Brett *Things could be worse*, pp. 77 – 90, Meanjin/Melbourne University Press, Carlton, Victoria, Australia, 1990.

Page 89: John Morrison, *Bushfire*, from: *Modern Australian Writing*, ed. Geoffrey Dutton, Collins, London, 1966.

Page 105: Roderick Finlayson, *The Totara Tree*, from: Roderick Finlayson, *Brown Man's Burden and Later Stories*, Auckland University Press/Oxford University Press, Auckland, New Zealand, 1973.

Page 114: Witi Ihimaera, *The Washerwoman's Children*, from: Witi Ihimaera *Dear Miss Mansfield*, pp. 181 – 191, Viking, Auckland, New Zealand, 1989.

Photographs

The material reproduced in this book has been taken from the following sources:
Australian Picture Library: page 57, 72 – Corbis GmbH, Düsseldorf: page 43 (Penny Tweedie), 88 (Jones Jon/ Corbis Sygma), 108 (Paul A. Souders) – Mitchell State Library: page 80 – National Library of Australia, Canberra: page 22, 23 – Alec Bolton, National Library of Australia: page 36, 49, 86 – John Oxley Library, Brisbane: page 28 – Robert Cross, Viking (Penguin) New Zealand: page 112 – Polyglott Verlag, München: page 8, 119 – Franz-Josef Thelen, Bergisch-Gladbach: cover – La Trobe Picture Collection, State Library of Victoria: page 18, 65 (Elizabeth Gilliam)